Treasure Hunt

Treasure Hunt
Copyright © 2016 by James A. Tweedie

Printed in USA by Dunecrest Press, Long Beach, WA 98631

LCCN 2016914873
ISBN 978-1-945539-06-0   eBook ISBN 978-1-945539-07-7

Treasure Hunt

One Week in the Life of
Mike Maurison
Private Eye

James A. Tweedie

Dunecrest Press

Table of Contents

Chapter One

Dessert

Saturday Evening

I love Mona with all my heart but I am not sure I will ever forgive her for accepting Aunt Lucille's dinner invitation. It's not that Aunt Lucille is a bad person or anything, it's just that our relationship carries more baggage than the basement of a 747.

Lucille is the only family I have left in the world. I suppose this is a point in her favor but the baggage is still there and it is all mine.

Mona on the other hand, likes Lucille and thinks I should stuff my baggage into an overhead compartment and leave it behind when I walk off the plane and into my aunt's house.

"Mona," I said, "that might work if we were on a plane but we're driving to Islip in Sid's car. Show me an overhead compartment and . . . ."

"Then shove it somewhere else," Mona interrupted *sans* her customary good humor. "At least while we're eating."

"I'll be good," I sighed, secretly hoping for a one-course meal and a short turn-around.

It had been a good day to live and breathe in Manhattan until we crossed the East River. Now, however, we were on our way to Aunt Lucille's. It was 5:30 p.m. on a Saturday afternoon in mid-September and my spirits were sagging more than the elastic in a pair of old underwear.

My mother disappeared when I was six and, once she was gone, my father never had anything good to say about my mother's older sister. As a result, when my father died twelve years later I decided I would have nothing to do with Aunt Lucille. We met at her husband's funeral last spring for the first time in 12 years. To my shame and embarrassment, she turned out to be a decent person. Since then I have tried to avoid her as much as possible.

It turned out the most awkward thing about getting married to Mona last July was sitting across from Aunt Lucille at the rehearsal dinner. Her two kids and grandchildren are nice enough but I would rather have been back in my office investigating a sewage plant explosion than driving to Islip.

"Nesbitt! Hello and welcome!" Lucille gushed as she opened the door to let us in.

No one calls me Nesbitt anymore except Aunt Lucille. To everyone else I am simply Mike . . . Mike Maurison—Private Eye.

"And Mona," she added. "I haven't seen either of you since the wedding."

Mona offered her hand and flashed her always-spectacular smile but instead of a handshake, Lucille grabbed her in a hug that would have gotten me a slap in the face if I had attempted it on a first date.

"Ben and Mindy and the kids couldn't make it but Connie is here. It's so nice we can be together again. I want to hear all about your honeymoon."

After that, there was no place for the evening to go but down.

After some wine and cheese accompanied by talk that was small enough to fit into a thimble we moved into second gear and started in on the salad course.

"How was the honeymoon?"

It sounded as if the conversation had been outlined in advance and was being read from a script. Mona, however, seemed ready to reveal every sordid detail of what had probably been the most dysfunctional honeymoon in history.

Fortunately, she skipped the parts about London, our new friend Du and the painting that may or may not be a Rembrandt. Trying to explain how I came to own something found in a trash bin that could be worth over $30 million if it turns out to be authentic would have taken more time than I wanted to spend with Aunt Lucille.

Mona quickly skipped ahead to describe the evening I was dumped behind a bush on top of a Swiss Alp after being kidnapped during an art robbery in Florence. I had, of course, heard it all before and knew my part of the story better than Mona, but I let her talk until the beef stroganoff was almost gone.

"Part of the trip was nice," I said in an attempt to shift the conversation in another direction. "But coming home was the best part."

When the conversation stalled out and Lucille disappeared into the kitchen to get cherry pie and ice cream I made the mistake of asking Connie what she was up to these days.

"I wish you hadn't asked," she said.

It wasn't long before I agreed with her.

"But since you did I might as well tell you."

What came next was a saga straight out of the *History Channel* or *Treasure Island*, or some movie that no one had ever heard of until Connie started telling us about it.

As Connie talked, Lucille ate her pie *alamode* but Mona and I were having such a hard time closing our mouths that our ice cream melted and our pies got soggy while we listened to the story unfold.

Connie lives in Brentwood just two miles from where we weren't eating our pie, but her story started just north of Albany where she was spending a weekend with Ben and Mindy. She had driven up to babysit Sam and Susan, her toddler nephew and niece, while their parents spent a romantic night in the Catskills.

Everything had gone along nicely until she was putting the kids to bed and the lights flickered out. Soon she heard sirens and a few minutes later the intersection down the street lit up like a theater marquee at a Hollywood premier. It turned out a large sinkhole had opened up in the middle of the street.

As she talked, I recalled reading something about it a day or so before we left on our honeymoon. Sinkholes happen in places like Florida all the time but in Albany, they are as rare as rooster eggs.

At first, everyone figured a water main had burst or a natural gas line had ruptured. Since no one could find any sign of gas and Old Faithful never started spurting everyone stood around scratching their heads and pretending they were busy rearranging the little orange traffic cones and yellow tape that had closed off the street.

After digging around the next morning, the repair crew finally figured out what had caused the cave-in. A well-placed phone call produced a couple of faculty members from the State University New York in Albany who were familiar with local history and archaeology. What they found was a tunnel. It was an old tunnel shored up with hand-cut timbers; timbers that had finally rotted out and collapsed under the weight of asphalt and traffic.

"I couldn't leave the kids alone to check it out when it happened," Connie said. "But in the morning we all walked down to see what was going on."

The whole thing turned out to be so interesting that Connie began soaking up everything she could find out about it.

Based on artifacts recovered from the bottom of the hole it was determined the tunnel dated back to the days of the French and Indian War in the mid-1700's. For all anyone could tell Major George Washington and Natty Bumppo could have slept there . . . assuming the tunnel had been built by the English. But the rusted lantern, broken pick axe and hand forged nails didn't have an accent so they could have just as easily been French.

When Connie drove home later in the afternoon that would have been the end of it except for what the archaeologists turned up next. When they got the debris cleared away they discovered that one end of the tunnel led to a manhole cover in a nearby vacant lot. In the other direction the tunnel led to a dead-end where they found 70 pounds of uncut cocaine worth $2.25 million, all neatly zipped up in a large pile of plastic baggies.

Connie's story would have made a good first chapter for a novel but there wasn't much more to it than that. The truth is, Mona and I would have already known most of it from the news media if we hadn't been busy chasing our tails around London, Paris, Florence and Rome when the story broke.

When Connie said, "But wait, I haven't got to the strange part, yet," Mona and I glanced at each other and started eating as much of our pie as we could before Connie started in again.

Connie paused to take a few bites of her own pie and then shifted the scene from Albany to the New York Public Library. The sinkhole in Albany had gotten her all fired up about the French and Indian War so she started spending her free time looking up books and articles that told all about the who, what, where, when, how and why of the whole imbroglio.

It seems that at the same moment I was involuntarily inhaling the cool, crisp air of the Swiss Alps, Connie was in the third floor Archives & Manuscripts section of the library flipping through an 18th century holographic journal written by a man named John Bedlow.

Bedlow had fought the French at the Battle of Lake George back in the day and had been thoughtful enough to write down what he had seen and heard during his sojourn in up-colony New York. Towards the end of the diary was an entry that mentioned a tunnel somewhere near Albany. The next few pages were missing and it looked as if someone had had cut them out with a blade.

"I was so frustrated," Connie said. "Here I had finally found a book that might have told me something about the tunnel and the punch line was missing. I carried the book over to the librarian to show him the damage. I expected him to be upset but all he did was start pushing the keys on his computer.

"After a few seconds he said, 'Here you go. It looks like we scanned it before the pages were cut. They're all here on-line if you want to read the rest of it.'

"I didn't have time but since there were only four or five pages left to read I asked if he could print them for me and he said that for twenty-five cents per page he would be happy to do it."

"Okay, Connie," I said as I took a casual and very conspicuous glance at my watch. "I'm sure there's more and I'm sure it's all interesting but it's getting late and we have to drive all the way back to the City before . . . ."

"No!" Connie said in as forceful a voice as she could manage without waking up the people next door. "You've got to hear the rest of it. You're a Private Investigator and I need you to hear this. Maybe you'll be able to figure it out. I've tried but . . . here, I'll try to keep it short."

She reached into her purse and pulled out a few sheets of neatly folded copier paper.

"Here is a copy of the last page I found in the book."

She had circled the following paragraph at the bottom of the page:

November 5, 1755. . . . Bloody Pond we returned with Captain Folsom to Ft. Lyman where we rest (sic) secured the stockade for ( ) weeks and where we remain. South on Mohawk a tunnel found with . . . .

"That's where the pages went missing. You can see how disappointing it was at the time. But there is sort of a happy ending," she added as she handed me the rest of the papers.

The next page of the book, now missing from the manuscript but printed from the computer, continued as follows:

. . . muskets, ball and powder dug by savage treachery as store perchance ( ) some plan to attack Albany.

"Good for you," I said, "and good sleuthing. Have you shared this with the folks up in Albany yet?"

"I was going to, but then," she paused and pointed to the right side margin of the missing page, "I noticed this."

I could see faint traces of words and scribbles as if drawn with invisible ink. With some effort, I made out the words "gld" and "bried hre" alongside a neatly drawn ✠ with an line pointing to the sentence at the top of the page; the sentence that appeared to refer to the tunnel just north of Albany.

"So?" I asked. "What's the point?"

I glanced over at Mona. She was so deep in conversation with Aunt Lucille that she probably had no idea how late it was getting.

"Don't you see?" Connie asked. "It's like a treasure map with buried gold like with pirates except it's not near the ocean but . . . you get the idea . . . don't you?"

"Sure, Connie, I see it. But I don't see what it has to do with me . . . or you for that matter. Just tell the people in Albany what you found and let them figure it out. Who knows, you might get mentioned in a Ken Burns documentary."

"It's *gold*, Mike, . . . and someone has already spotted the clue and cut the pages out of the book and for all we know he . . . or she . . . is up in Albany right now with a metal detector trying to hit the lottery. I don't know about you but I hate coming in second place."

"Then go and buy a metal detector and give it your best shot," I suggested. "But leave me out. I've got other fried fish to . . . uh . . . to fry."

"Then that's it? You're done with the story? I thought you'd jump at the chance to take on a real case like Indiana Jones or like in a Dan Brown novel. And I didn't even get to the good part yet."

"Later," I said. "Maybe later."

"Mona," I added. "It's past my bedtime. It's time to say "Goodnight" and go home."

I stood up and said, "It's been fun. Thanks for the food and everything. It's nice to see you again. Come on, Mona. Let's go."

Mona leaned over and whispered something in Lucille's ear. They both looked at me and started laughing.

"Okay, Mike," Mona said as she stood up. "I'm ready to go now."

Turning back she added, "I'm glad we came. Maybe you could come over to our place some time?"

I had promised Mona I would be nice but as far as I was concerned, she was carrying the nice thing further than necessary.

"Let's go," I said for the third and final time.

Mona gave a little wave to Aunt Lucille and blew a kiss to Connie as we stepped onto the porch on our way to the car.

Thank god, I said to myself, *we're finally out of there.*

But Connie wasn't done with me yet.

"Mike," I heard her say quietly as she followed me down the steps. "The gold was never in the tunnel."

I turned around and looked her straight in the eyes. There was an awkward moment when I couldn't think of anything to say; so I turned my back to her, got in the car and drove home with Mona.

All I could think about was gold.

Chapter Two

Sri Lanka
Sunday Morning

After a leisurely breakfast together, Mona headed off to church and I headed over to my office to meet with a client. After we got married, we moved nine blocks north so I don't see my old neighbors and friends as often as I used to. Feeling nostalgic, I dropped by my old corner store to grab a cup of coffee and see Juan who runs the place.

"*¡Hola!*" I said in the best-bastardized Spanish I could scrape up on the spur of the moment. "*Com savvi?*" I added in my worst-bastardized French.

"Same to you." Juan replied, adding the caveat, "What you said . . . I think."

There was a pause.

"So," he continued. "You are still married man, *si?*"

"*Si*," I replied as I handed him some cash. "Keep the change."

Juan's English may be rough around the edges but he seems to have no problem understanding the universal language of *dinero*.

"Keep the money," he said as he handed it back. "It's on my house because you are my friend and I congratulate all of you."

"Thank you and *gracias*," I said redundantly. "It's good to see you again. *Ciao*."

"*Saluto il vostro marito*," he replied with a smile as I walked out the door.

We may not understand what we say to each other but we understand each other well enough to say it.

"Hi, Bergie," I waved as I walked up the stairs to my building.

Bergie was unlocking the door to her beauty salon, a four-seater ladies remodling center that doubles as a conservatory of fine facial art on the ground floor beneath my office.

Bergie replied with a wave as I stepped up the pace to make sure I got to the office before my client did.

At nine-thirty sharp the door buzzer went off and I buzzed back to let the guy in.

"Mr. Maurison?" he asked as he stuck his head into my office.

"That's what it says on the door, so you might as well come in and choose a chair," I said, pointing at the only chair in the room besides my own.

"What's the deal?" I asked, coming to the point as sharply as I could. "You've got the cards so what's the game?"

The guy looked around as if he might have walked into the wrong room by mistake.

After a reflective moment he looked back at me and said, "I want to play hide and seek and I want you to show me how to do it."

"Sure, I can do that," I said, " and I'll throw in 'Ring Around the Rosie' and 'Capture the Flag' for free if you'll tell me what in the world you're talking about?"

"It's my wife," he said.

I have heard that line a million times along with its genetically modified sibling: "It's my husband." They both mean the same thing. Someone suspects there is an affair going on. If it was just irreconcilable differences or being mad at each other they would be seeing a counsellor instead of a private eye. With me it's always an affair.

"So," I said, "what's up with your wife and what does she have to do with the 'Hide and Seek' thing?"

I knew exactly what he was going to say but I was wrong.

"I love my wife with all my heart," he said, "and she loves me. Too much, I think. She's always going out of her way to buy me greeting cards and at least once a week there is a love note stuck on my mirror in the morning or on the milk container in the refrigerator. She tries to meet my every need—and I do mean my every need. She is a great cook and every evening she manages to come up with something new and wonderful. It's always healthy with fresh, organic vegetables, meat from hormone-free cattle and coffee from a free-trade store down the street.

"She recycles everything, rides a bicycle or walks everywhere, keeps our apartment spotlessly clean and raised our two children into successful, well-educated professionals with strong, happy marriages. She volunteers with the local Food for Kids backpack program to help schoolchildren whose families are short of cash and now that our own kids are gone she works thirty hours a week on-line with an international retail distributor headquartered in Hong Kong. She makes more money than I do."

While he paused to catch his breath I was imagining that all of this must be driving him nuts. How in the world could any normal guy keep up with a gal like that?

"It's all wonderful, of course," he said as my latest theory crumbled into dust. "I must be the luckiest guy in the world.

"Everything I do for her . . . like flowers or dinner out or a Saturday matinee at a Broadway show . . . it doesn't matter . . . whatever I do she acts as giddy as a junior high school girl holding hands with a boy for the first time. She is sweet and kind and keeps a pet gerbil and two parakeets because we're not allowed to have a dog in our flat . . . . "

"Excuse me," I inturruped. "Back when you came in I asked you about your wife and what she had to do with the "Hide and Seek" thing? Since then you've sort of told me about the wife but . . . ."

"Just hold it a moment," he interrupted back at me. "I'm almost there."

I glanced at my watch, wishing I was a cab driver parked at a curb with the meter running, waiting for a passenger to finish talking on their phone.

"Okay," I said. "Finish it up but get to the point."

"What I'm trying to say is that Monica; that's my wife . . . I'm Chet, by the way . . . but I already told you that on the phone . . . ."

I glanced at my watch again and wondered why the second hand was moving so slowly.

"What I'm trying to say," he repeated, "is that I'm having an affair and I don't want my wife to find out about it."

Then he stopped talking.

Finally.

He put his hands behind his head, leaned back in his chair as far as he could without falling over

17

backwards, and flashed me the widest, happiest smile I have ever seen outside of old Shirley Temple movies.

"Excuse me?" I asked, suddenly wondering if I needed testing for a hearing aid.

"Oh, I know what you're thinking but you've got it all wrong," he said.

I wasn't clear about what I got wrong but if he was right then it was strike three and I was out. If I had been an Old Testament prophet, I would have been stoned to death for failure to perform.

"Remember the old chewing gum commercial?" Chet asked. "The one that said, 'Double your pleasure, double your fun?' You know the one I mean? Well it's true. Monica is perfect and I am perfectly happy with her but now I've got two Monicas and everything is twice as perfect. It might be hard for you to understand but I'm twice as happy as I was before!"

"Uh, Chet?" I asked. "What does Monica think about this? I mean either or both of them?"

"Neither of them knows about the other and that's what makes it so perfect. They both love me so much that they trust me completely. I could add a third or fourth Monica and neither of them would ever suspect anything, but just in case, that's why I'm here talking to you."

"Oh," I said, wondering whether I should be scratching my head like those first responders to the sinkhole in Albany or moving little orange cones around to keep Chet at a safe distance.

"I need to come up with a plan," he went on. "You know, some way to keep the whole thing a secret so no one finds out about it. If anyone did, it would be a disaster. Right now all of us are happy and in love and I'd like to keep it that way, so . . . can you help me with some tips to help me 'hide' so they won't 'go seek?'"

I glared at him through cold, squinty eyes.

With as much disgust in my voice as I could muster I asked, "Let me get this straight. You're asking me to help you lie, cheat and deceive both your wife and your lover so all three of you can be happy?"

"Yes," he said with a chuckle. "That's exactly right. I figured that private eyes are good at being sneaky and sleuthy and stuff like that. You've probably been hired a hundred times to spy on husbands and wives and you probably know what's worked well for them and where they've screwed up and got busted.

"Whatever your hourly fee is I'll pay you double if you'll help me with the plan. Let's start by going over my weekly schedule and see how I can juggle the . . . ."

"No deal," I said. "I may have anted up but now that I've seen the cards I'm throwing them in and folding. The game's over. Take your chips and slither home to your slime ball life without me. And you owe me fifty dollars for my time."

The slob sat staring at me in disbelief.

"I thought you were a pro," he said as he counted out the cash. "I didn't know I was getting hooked up with a puritanical, self-righteous, narrow-minded, judgmental, bigoted prude."

There was another brief pause before he spoke again.

"No offense intended," he said. "By the way, if that's how you feel could you refer me to someone who *would* be willing to help me out? I'd really appreciate it. I only have another hour or two before I have to get home to Monica and I'd like to get the ball rolling, if you know what I mean."

"Get out of my office," I said quietly, standing up and trying to look as menacing as possible.

I doubt if my six-foot tall, slightly paunchy stature intimidated him much but he seemed to take the hint. Without looking back or saying a word, he walked out of the room and disappeared into the fog of his personal world of fantasy and science fiction.

I was tempted to rub hand sanitizer all over his chair and spray the rest of the room with disinfectant but decided that whatever moral disease he had was probably not contagious.

A year ago, I might have accepted his offer but that was before I was totally hooked on Mona. I guess without knowing it she has tamed me in the same way a pet owner turns a feral cat into a domesticated one. Some of Mona's sense of right and wrong has burrowed into me as well, oozing into my conscience in ways that occasionally catch me off guard.

Like just now, for example.

The thought of someone cheating on Mona must have pushed me over the edge. Moral indignation is a new feeling and a new experience for me and I was surprised to discover how good it felt when I threw Chet to the wolves. It had been the right thing to do, of course. After all, he was one of them.

After Chet was out of the way there was still unfinished business sitting on my desk. There were phone calls to make and a report on a case I needed to write up for a client. Instead of doing my duty, however, I stood up, locked the door behind me and walked home to be with my one and only Mona.

I stopped to buy a single red rose from a street-corner vendor and wondered if it would make Mona as "giddy as a junior high school girl" when I gave it to her. The thought passed quickly, though, because I knew I hadn't bought the flower to make Mona feel giddy. I bought it because . . . well . . . I guess I bought it because it was going to make me feel giddy to give it to her.

Mona and I arrived at the street entrance to our building at the same moment.

"What? No football game on TV this morning?" she teased, knowing full well I had been at my office.

"There were lots of them on TV this morning," I said. "There were so many replays reviewed by the officials that the game I watched was over in 20 minutes,"

"By the way," I added as an afterthought. "Did you hear what happened in Sri Lanka last night?"

"No," Mona replied with a puzzled look on her face. "What happened?"

"I have no idea," I said. "I was hoping you might know. That's why I asked."

Mona didn't say anything.

After rolling her eyes around in an arctic circle, she handed me the two bags of groceries she was carrying and silently walked into the building without me.

When I caught up with her at the third floor entrance to our flat, I put the groceries on the floor, pulled the rose out of a piece of rolled newspaper and handed it to her saying, "Sweets for the sweet—and there is nothing sweeter than a red rose . . . except for you!"

I thought it was romantic and spontaneous and I was expecting to feel giddy.

Instead, Mona took the flower, and after picking off an imperfect petal said, "Did you hear what happened to the person who asked what happened in Sri Lanka last night?"

"No," I said, playing along. "What happened?"

"I have no idea," she answered.

She walked into the apartment; grabbed a small vase from the cupboard; filled it with water; placed the rose in it, and put them both in the center of the dining table.

As I set the groceries on the kitchen counter Mona said, "Did you hear what happened in church this morning?"

"No," I said, not sure if I should keep playing along or not. "What happened?"

"How nice of you to ask," she said. "I wasn't sure you were interested but since you want to know I'll tell you.

"Pastor Cheryl announced she is leaving in two weeks. She said her mother has been in poor health and her brother, who has kept an eye on her in Cincinnati for the past ten years, is moving to Madrid, the one in Spain. Her mother isn't able to go with him and she would rather die than move to Manhattan. This means that she is either going to move into assisted living or someone is going to have to call time out and move in with her until someone comes up with a better solution.

"Pastor Cheryl said that the 'someone' who is going to have to call time out, the 'someone' who is going to have to move in with her mother and the 'someone' who is going to come up with a better solution is going to be her. Not forever, she says, but for at least six months.

"'It's a leave of absence,' she explained. 'I'll be back in time for Easter.'"

"Six months is long time," I said, "but I'm glad she's coming back. She's the only preacher I ever heard that made any sense. And since she's the one who married us I want her to stick around in case we need a tune up or something to keep our marriage warranty up to date."

"I've got a better idea," Mona suggested. "Why don't you come to church with me next Sunday. That way you can tell her what you just told me. After all, you might actually be on to something. I've never thought of Cheryl as being a spiritual auto mechanic before. The next time you start squeaking I'll take you in for a lube job."

"Mona," I asked, feeling the need to get serious for a moment. "Are you okay with this? Cheryl has been your go-to church person for a long time. What's going to happen when she's not around?"

"Life will go on with or without her, I guess. Pastor Palmer will share the preaching with some guest speakers and other than that, things will be about the same. Besides, now that I'm married, you can be my spiritual go-to person if I need one."

"Don't get your hopes up," I warned. "You know how I feel about prayer and religious stuff. I'm not any good at it. Maybe you could watch Billy Graham on TV?"

"Billy Graham is retired," Mona said. "He's old and doesn't come on TV any more."

"Then watch Robert Schuller."

"Schuller is dead and doesn't come on TV any more either."

"Then how about that guy Kennedy or whoever he is from that church in Florida. You could watch him."

"He died, too." Mona said. "So I guess I'm stuck with you. The Bible says you're supposed to be my "help-meet" in faith as well as life. So here's your chance."

"Help you meet who?" I asked with a smile and a wink, trying to put a lighthearted spin onto a conversation that was getting seriously beyond my comfort level.

"Mike," she answered. "I don't need Pastor Cheryl and I don't need to meet anyone but you. You have more faith inside you than you think. I wouldn't have married you if I wasn't sure of it. Think about it. Pray about it. Pray about it any way you like. Use words if you have to. Just talk to God about it and come to church with me next Sunday—for Pastor Cheryl. Okay?"

All I could muster was a shrug and a "Sure, whatever you say."

25

Mona walked over, put her arms around me, gave me a soft kiss on the lips and said, "Thank you for the flower."

I looked around but if there was any giddiness in the room, I must have missed it.

Chapter Three

Obsessive Compulsive
Sunday Afternoon

I helped Mona pull the groceries out of the bags. The first thing I grabbed was a tin of sardines.

"What is this for?" I asked.

"Lunch."

"Whose lunch."

"Ours."

"Why?"

"Because I like sardines and you will too if you want me to fix you lunch."

Since I don't like sardines just as much as I don't like eggplant I had no choice but to graciously surrender all of the sardines to Mona and scrounge around the fridge for leftovers.

I had corralled a half-empty bag of baby carrots and a jar of peanut butter when my phone rang. It was Connie.

"Hi, Connie," I said, hoping she had misdialed.

"Mike," she asked. "Are you at home right now?"

"Yes, but why do you care?"

"Because I'm two blocks away on Lexington and I'll be there in five minutes."

I started to make up a lie about how busy I was but she had already hung up.

As I absent-mindedly stuck a carrot in the peanut butter jar, I mentioned to Mona that Connie was coming over. When Mona saw me stick the same half-eaten carrot back into the jar for a second time she announced that from now on we would have *His* and *Hers* peanut butter jars.

"I have enough saliva of my own," was how she put it.

The intercom buzzed. I knew it was Connie so I buzzed her in without waiting to talk.

Two minutes later Connie was sitting on our sofa pulling the neatly folded papers out of her purse again.

"This can't wait," she decreed as if she was Catherine the Great asserting the divine right of tyrants.

"When you left my Mom's place last night I told you the gold had never been in the cave. Didn't that make you curious? Just a little?"

"No," I lied. "Why would that interest me?"

"Because I think I know where the gold is . . . or where it *was*. I don't know if it is still there or not, but I'd like to find out and I'm not comfortable going to look for it by myself. I want you to go with me."

She paused and looked over at Mona.

Mona tried to keep a straight face but the laughter broke out against her best efforts.

"What's so funny?" Connie asked. "I don't get it?"

"Because," Mona said gasping for air, "it doesn't matter if Mike wants to go with you or not. It doesn't matter if you're looking for the treasure of the Sierra Madre or the lost continent of Atlantis. If something is lost and someone asks Mike to find it he's obsessive-compulsive enough to say yes every time; especially if there's a contract that includes expenses. As a bonus, he won't stop looking until he either finds it or gets fired. Am I right, dear?"

"You're right about the compulsive part but at the moment my only obsession is being in love with you."

"Ahhh, that's so sweet!" Connie sighed. "But are you compulsive enough to go on a treasure hunt with me?"

"That depends on what else you've got in those papers."

She walked over to the dining table and laid the pages side by side.

29

"Here's the page that's still in the book," she explained, "the one where I circled the paragraph where the tunnel is first mentioned."

"And here's the copy of the first missing page with the extra writing on it."

Since I was now sitting at the table, Connie slid the page in my direction and pointed at the marginal squiggles.

"Here's the line that went from the ✠ to the top sentence on the page, remember?"

"Sure, of course. What about it?"

"We thought it was an arrow telling us that the "bried gld" was in the tunnel, right?"

I nodded.

"But we were wrong. It isn't an arrow at all. It's just a line. See? There's no pointy arrow thingy at the end of it. It just scribbles up and stops there like a dead end."

"If it's not an arrow then what is it?" I asked showing a spark of interest for the first time.

"It's a river, or a road," Connie replied. "The whole thing's a map. The ✠ is where the gold is and it's somewhere along the squiggly line. The other markings seem to be numbers and other notes too faint to decipher. It's too bad we don't have the original. It's probably clear enough to read."

"So how do the lines and numbers tell you where the gold is?" I asked.

"They don't," she said. "The journal does."

She pointed to the short paragraph next to the ✠. It was the second entry after the comment about the tunnel.

"I told you," she continued, "Ben and Mindy's place is half-way between Albany and Schenectady just below the Mohawk River. That's where the tunnel is. The writer was twenty miles north at Ft. Lyman when he mentioned it. Later they renamed it Ft. Edwards but that doesn't matter because in the next few entries he's in Massachusetts."

December the 14th—All New Hampshire ordered home but for Cpt. Rogers company. Pray be w/wife & family for Christmas. ( ) snow forced South to Albany and below Green Mts. to Worcester & North.

December the 19th—Ordered halt nr Worcester on French R. to guard quary. (✠) Two days lost for why?

December 25th—Christmas and home to family & fire. God be thankit for my (sic) delverence.

"See?" she pointed. "The ✠ is next to the words 'French R.' All we have to do is find a quarry and match it up with the map. The line must be the French River, right? So the gold is there. Or was there . . . I think."

There was a long pause before she continued.

"Maybe this is just too weird. Maybe I'm too weird and I'm making this whole thing up. I'm sorry, Mike. I guess I got carried away. I'm just fooling myself. Why would there be gold in Worcester, Massachusetts in the middle of nowhere in 1755? None of it makes sense. I must be nuts."

She stood up, pulled the papers together and added, "I'll be going now. Sorry to bother you on a Sunday."

Most of me agreed with her about the "must be nuts" conclusion but a small part of me was beginning to see some sense in what she was talking about. The whole business of colonial gold was a long shot by a long shot but if for some strange reason it was true, then the odds against it didn't really matter one way or the other. Gold is gold and true is true.

That's when my compulsive disorder kicked in.

"Uh, Connie?" I found myself saying. "Don't leave. I think you might be on to something."

I caught a glimpse of Mona. She was standing in the kitchen rolling her eyes again. She did a poor imitation of a smile, shook her head slowly side-to-side, walked into the bedroom and closed the door behind her. She knew I was hooked . . . and so did I.

The first thing Connie and I did was find a good map of New England.

We traced a pencil line from Lake George to Ft. Edwards to Albany. From there we followed I-90 east until it crossed the small, winding French River just a few miles west of Worcester, Massachusetts.

When Connie marked a small "X" on the map, I felt the need to talk to Mona.

"Would you mind if Connie and I drove up to Massachusetts for a couple of days . . . you know, just to check this out and get it out of our system?"

Mona, who was lying on the bed reading the newspaper looked up and shrugged.

"Do what you have to do, but remember: time is money. Unless you find a pot of gold at the end of the rainbow this thing with Connie is going to cost more than we can afford."

"I guess that means you're okay with it," I said with more than a hint of sarcasm.

"If you started with three guesses then you have two of them left," she mumbled as she turned her attention back to the newspaper.

"Connie," I said when I emerged from the bedroom. "Let's go up to Worcester tomorrow and snoop around. I can cancel my morning appointment and if you're free, we could drive up and be back by dinner. Why put off until tomorrow what you can do today?"

"Mike, you're more compulsive than I thought, but what you said makes sense. Why wait until tomorrow? I drove into town with my car this morning. That means we can leave right now if you want. I'm free and I don't want to make another round trip to Brentwood unless I have to. As I said, I don't like to finish in second place. It's gold we're after; not silver."

Mona didn't say anything when I told her our plans but she was thoughtful enough to fix each of us a late-lunch snack to eat on the way.

I grabbed a change of clothes, Mona loaned Connie a few unmentionables and off we went.

As we were crossing the East River on the RFK Bridge, I opened my snack bag and pulled out a slice of dry bread and a tin of sardines.

Inside Connie's bag was an apple, a bottle of water, a baggie filled with animal crackers and a note that said, "Connie: It must be genetic. Hopefully someone will find a cure. Mona."

I ate the bread.

By 2:30, we were south of Hartford, Connecticut buying gas with one hour of driving left before we hit Worcester. Connie stayed in the car while I filled the tank.

A red Mazda Miata pulled up next to us. I noticed Connie turn her head, stare at the driver and duck out of sight, but not quickly enough.

"Connie!" he cried as he climbed out and walked over to where my cousin had hunched down in the driver's seat. "Wow! It's good to see you!"

Connie sat up and lowered the window.

"Hi Joe," she blushed. "I dropped my keys. What are you doing in Hartford?"

"I was about to ask you the same question," he laughed. "It's been a long time."

His smile disappeared, replaced with a glare that could have shattered bricks.

Connie glanced at me as if to say, *Leave the tank half empty if you have to, but get me out of here . . . now!*

I pulled the nozzle out of the tank, screwed the cap on and climbed into the passenger seat without waiting for a receipt.

"Hey, Joe," I smiled across the car. "I'm Mike. Connie and I are late for an appointment. Nice to meet you but we've got to go . . . ."

"Not so fast," Joe said as he leaned into the car. "Connie and I have some things to discuss, don't we?"

Connie turned towards me with eyes that were starting to leak at the corners.

With a sigh she said, "Mike, can you wait here just a minute? You can pull the car over to a parking place if you need to. I'll be right back."

Connie and Joe walked over to the Miata, climbed in and drove away.

I was still in a car but thanks to Connie, I was also in a lurch. Since there was nothing I could do about it, I climbed into the driver's seat and drove the car over to a normal parking spot.

Back in high school, I had a friend who tried his hand at poetry. The best he could come up with was a couplet that went like this:

When in danger, when in doubt,
Run in circles; scream and shout.

I thought it was clever and actually carried it around in my wallet for several years. As I grew older and wiser, however, I learned it was not very good advice. In its place, I created Mike's Survival Rule #1: "When in danger—Run," immediately followed by Mike's Survival Rule #2: "When in doubt—Stay where you are."

Rules are made to be broken, of course, and I have broken Rule #2 several times over the years. Each time it turned out it would have been better if I had stayed put. So . . . while keeping my eyes open for Connie I sat in the car and waited . . . and waited . . . and waited . . . until she finally showed up around 3:45 p.m.

Connie and Joe got out of the Miata, met at the rear of the car, wrapped each other in an embrace that made Aunt Lucille's look G-Rated and kissed as if they would never kiss again. When the display of affection was over, they stepped apart and stood facing each other for a few moments. Connie whispered something I couldn't hear, and then turned and began walking in my direction. Joe got into the Miata and drove away.

"Mike, what are you doing sitting around like a bump on a log?" Connie asked as she came up to the car. "'We're off to Great Places! Today is our day! Our mountain is waiting. So . . . let's get on our way!'"

"Dr. Seuss, right?" I asked.

"Sort of," she replied, and then after a brief pause she added, "We don't have all day. Give me the keys."

I didn't bother to ask her about Joe.

We arrived in Worcester a few minutes before 5:00 p.m. and turned west on US 20 heading towards the French River two miles down the road.

The French River is neither long nor wide. It is, in fact, more of a drainage than a river as it meanders through trees with intermittent stops at ponds along the way to its junction with the Quinebaug River about 15 miles south of where we were.

It was already late in the day and we had to decide whether to follow the river north, or south. To save time we stopped to buy gas and ask a few questions.

The teenage girl in the mini-mart was friendly enough. "If you mean a quarry where they cut rock to make buildings then 'No', there isn't one of those, but if you mean like for gravel, there's one just up the road towards WalMart. "

"How long has it been there," Connie asked.

"I have no idea," the girl answered. "I suppose it's been there since before I was born."

We backtracked half a mile and checked out the place. It was a broad, dusty area where exposed rock had been scraped off by bulldozers. If it had been a "quary" back in Bedlow's day it wouldn't have been of much use to anybody or a place important enough to have someone guard it.

Since everything was nearby, we drove two miles north where the French River first flows out of a pond. Except for scattered warehouses, a golf course, and some nice homes there wasn't much to see.

Heading south, we stopped nearly every mile, asking about quarries or local stories about the French and Indian War. When we mentioned the word "gold", people's eyes got a little bigger but no one had anything to tell us.

To save time we drove south into Connecticut where the French River disappears into the Quinebaug, made a u-turn, and started working our way back.

No one we talked to knew anything and we didn't notice anything of interest until just south of Oxford when I shouted, "Stop, Connie, stop!"

Just to the right, off the road hidden by a line of trees was a rocky outcrop with the French River lapping on the north side. Some of the stone appeared to have been cut but it didn't look like much had happened there for a long time. Was this the quarry? Was gold still buried there?

We drove around the area asking people about the quarry but no one could tell us anything about it. In fact, only one of them even knew it was there.

It was getting late so we drove into Oxford looking for a place to eat.

There were a number of places that looked as if they could serve up a decent meal. Eventually we settled on one called "The Pepper Onion."

Chapter Four

Quary
Sunday Evening

Our waitress was named "Judy," at least that's what it said on her name tag and when I called her "Judy" she didn't seem surprised.

"Judy," I said as she was taking our order. "We're looking for an old stone quarry somewhere around here; one that dates back to the colonial times. Do you happen to know anything about it?"

"No, I can't say that I do," she said. "There's a rocky place down the road that looks like somebody might have chopped it up a little but that was back during the depression when they were building roads all over the place and needed some gravel. I guess you could call it a quarry but that would be a stretch."

"Well," I said as I handed her my business card, "if you ever think of something give me a call. We're working on a historical survey and it would be an important part of our paper if we could find it."

Connie ordered a Chicken Caesar Salad and I had meat loaf. If my Mom had ever made meat loaf, the Pepper Onion's would have been almost as good as hers.

When we had swallowed everything we wanted to digest, we had a debriefing.

"Maybe we were thrown off by the word 'quary,'" I suggested. "After all it could mean something besides a place where you excavate rocks or gravel."

"Like what?" Connie asked.

"Well, a 'quarry' could be a hunted animal or a person who is being chased and a 'quarrel' is an argument or maybe a type of arrow and that makes me think of Mohawks . . ."

"None of that makes sense," Connie interjected, "unless the man was ordered to guard captured prisoners or wild animals."

"I doubt it was animals but the prisoner idea has possibilities."

"There is something else I just thought of," Connie added. "We should have thought of it right away but we've been assuming the writer of the journal was the same person who drew the map in the margin. What if it was someone else? Maybe it was drawn a hundred years later?"

"There aren't a lot of words or letters to compare," I mused. "The ink seems different but it's impossible to tell without the original page. We could be wrong about it being a map, too, and we could be wrong about the buried gold having something to do with the French River."

Connie carried the conversation to the next level.

"Since you mention it, we could even be wrong about what the letters "gld bried hre" stand for. Maybe it is short for "golden bried" like a cheese with a 'd' . . . ."

"Or," I continued, "it could be 'brandied glider' or 'guild' or 'gland' and none of that makes sense either."

"It could be the word 'guilder' and that would make sense. Personally, I think we might be right about the 'buried gold,' Connie added, "but everything else is a complete mess."

"Well," I summarized. "It looks as if we're back to the beginning."

"Actually," Connie replied, "we're back to before the beginning. We'll have to find out where to start all over again."

"Or give it all up and go home," I said, looking at my watch. "It's 8:00 p.m., we don't have a hotel room and if we headed back now we wouldn't get to Manhattan 'til around 12:30 a.m. and I'm too tired to help you drive."

Our waitress came by to ask if we wanted more coffee.

"No, thanks," we both said at the same time.

"Just bring the bill," I said.

"Can you recommend a place to stay for the night?" Connie asked as the waitress turned to walk away."

She paused to turn back and say, "There are a couple of hotels where I-395 meets I-90 and some more just south of where I-90 hits I-84. Those are the closest I can think of. I can't say if any of them are good or not."

We had already decided Connie would pay for the gas, I would pay for the food and each of us would pay for our own lodging if we needed it. It looked as though we were going to need the lodging.

With twilight to our left, we headed back the way we came. When we got to US 20 we turned east towards I-395 where we found a Comfort Inn at a reasonable price.

"So," I asked, thinking about what Mona said about our finances, "how about we share a room? Two queen beds would save us both a lot of dough. It's not as if we're 'kissing cousins' or anything."

"Are you crazy? I'm sure Mona wouldn't approve and, kissing cousins or not, I don't like the idea, either. We'll get two separate rooms . . . unless you want to sleep in the car to save a few dollars."

"Sure, whatever," I said with resignation.

I had only brought twenty dollars cash so the credit card was going to have to fill in for a fat wallet. We were out of state so the ATM machine was going to cost extra, too. I could predict that Mona was going to say 'I told you so' as soon as I walked in the door the next day . . . or the day after that.

My compulsive disorder was scrambling my common sense into an omelet. Like Mona said, if something is lost I'll keep looking for it until I either find it or get fired. At the moment, the only person who could fire me was Connie and she didn't look as if she was in any hurry to head home either. This was turning into a longer trip than I had planned.

We said "Good night" and each of us promised to bring a Plan B to the coffee shop at breakfast the next morning

The letter "B" has always been one of my favorites but that night I couldn't think of a single plan to attach to it.

Chapter Five

Plan B

Monday Morning

At breakfast, we sat at the counter hoping we would get served more quickly than at a table. After ordering and getting our coffee, we were ready to start a new day.

"What's your Plan B?" I asked.

"Plan B is to assume the marginal drawing is a map of buried gold but not necessarily related to the French River or a quarry. I can't decide if the journal writer drew the map or someone else did. If it is a map, the line must be a river or a road but the only clues we have are in the journal and I'm not getting any inspiration from it.

"What about you?"

I took a leisurely sip of coffee as I thought about it. Then I added some cream and sugar and stirred the cup for as long as I could until I saw that Connie was getting impatient.

"Plan B," I finally said, "is to call it quits and head home."

"That's not a Plan B," Connie said. "That's a towel thrown into the ring by a quitter."

"You didn't give me a chance to finish. Plan B is to go home but I also have a Plan C."

"Which is . . . ?"

"Connie, I agree with you that the stuff in the margin is a map and I don't think it's contemporary with the journal, either. My guess is that it was drawn long after the French and Indian War but I think it clearly has something to do with what's written in the journal. I think there is a clue about the gold's location in the text but there are too many places to choose from. After all, at that point in the journal the trail goes from Lake George to Ft. Edwards to Albany, then along the Boston road to Worcester with a stop at a quarry next to the French River and then north to the man's home in New Hampshire.

"Somewhere along that route is a squiggly line where someone once buried some gold."

"That's not a 'plan,'" Connie said. "That's a commentary. A plan is where you suggest we do something."

"As far as doing something is concerned, your plan wasn't very helpful, either," I countered.

"So then," Connie said quietly, "it's over. Neither of us can think of anything to do and we can't spend the rest of our lives looking for a squiggly line in a New England haystack. I vote for your Plan B. Let's go home. If something comes up, we can always give it another try. What do you say—'Yes' or 'No'?"

"I say let's go home."

So we did.

Connie dropped me at my office at Noon and went home to Long Island.

I had already texted Mona what we were doing and she had texted me back with, "*Mike, Your turn to fix dinner. 7:00 p.m. sharp. It had better be good. I love you anyway. Mona.*"

Married bliss.

Chapter Six

Sweet Stop
Monday Afternoon

I phoned the client I had cancelled so we could set up another appointment. He said he had the afternoon free and could come in at 2:30 p.m. if my schedule was clear. It was, so we agreed on the time.

I had just hung up and was thinking about lunch when my cell phone started playing *Bolero*.

"Hello?" came a voice from a number in Massachusetts, "Is this Mike Maurison?"

"That's what it says on my credit card," I said with a sinking feeling as I remembered how much I had just spent on it.

"That's what it says on the business card I'm holding, too. What a coincidence. Are you the guy who was asking about the French River in my restaurant yesterday evening?"

That explained the Massachusetts phone number.

"Yes," I said. "I was asking about it yesterday. Who are you and why are you calling me?"

"I'm Ralph LaPointe, Manager of the Pepper Onion Restaurant in New Oxford. Did you happen to eat here last night?"

"I did. What's that to you?"

"Nothing, really, except curiosity. Judy, the waitress who took your card, told me you'd been asking about quarries along the French River. She says she told you she didn't know anything about it. She may not know about it but I do. There isn't one. At least not one that amounts to anything or dates back to the colonial days you were talking about yesterday."

"How do you know so much about this?" I asked.

"Because I was born and raised on the north end of the river and have spent the rest of my life here on the south end. I know every step of it, but that's not why I phoned you.

"Like I just said, I'm curious about something. Three days ago a young women ate lunch here and asked me the exact same question: 'Is there a quarry somewhere on the French River?' I gave her the same answer I gave you but maybe you can tell me what's going on? Why all the sudden interest in a quarry?"

As they say, my interest was piqued.

"Uh," I stammered, "Tell me about the woman and I'll tell you about the quarry thing. Did she have a name? Do you know where she was from or anything else about her?"

"I don't know. She might have been in her late 20s or early 30s. She was sitting down so it's hard to figure how tall she was; probably around my wife's height which is five foot seven. She had short black hair with bangs and was wearing clothes like a motorcyclist; you know what I mean, leather jacket and pants, thick leather boots, but no tattoos I could see."

"Is that all?"

"She sounded like someone from the Bronx or maybe Queens . . . somewhere down around New York or Manhattan. I could be wrong but that's what I think she sounded like. Oh, and she had some old papers with writing on them. She showed me one page that had a map on the edge. She said she thought it might be the French River and asked if I recognized what section of the river it might be. She kept her thumb over part of the map as though there was something she didn't want me to see."

"I told her to forget it. If that scribbled line was the French River then the only person who could tell her about it was the person who drew it and, from the looks of the paper, that person must have died a long time ago."

"That's all I know," he said. "Now it's your turn. What's this all about? It's probably something trivial but I've lived here all my life and questions like this one pique my curiosity."

It struck me as funny how words you never hear or think about suddenly show up like a flock of geese. We were both "piqued" like the top of a mountain but that wasn't the point.

"I'm researching some history about the French and Indian War," I explained." I'm particularly interested in the year 1755 when Worcester was starting to turn into a town. Recently I read a journal written by a soldier who wrote he had been assigned to guard a quarry along the French River on his way home to New Hampshire from the Battle of Lake George. I thought it might be interesting if I could find the quarry he mentioned in his journal. That's all. I could be wrong about the whole thing but I thought I'd check it out. I'm a curious sort of guy, too, and as far as who that lady was, or why she was asking about the same things, I have absolutely no idea. Maybe the pages she showed you were from the same journal. I don't know. But I'd sure like to track her down and find out."

I counted to six before Massachusetts replied, "Sorry I can't help you with the quarry question, but thanks for the explanation. It's an interesting story; one I've never heard before. I'll probably ask around about it just out of, you know . . . ."

". . . curiosity," I finished the sentence for him.

"Yeah . . . curiosity. Take care and stop by the next time you're in New Oxford."

I immediately phoned Connie.

"So, what do we do now?" I asked after I brought her up to speed.

"It sounds like this lady's a few steps ahead of us but she apparently drew the same blank we did at French River. The question is where is she going next and does she know something we don't?"

"I don't really care where she's going next," I countered. "What I want to know is where *we're* going next."

"I wish I knew who she is," Connie said. "She may be our competition but she could also turn out to be a partner in solving this thing. At least we know where the missing journal pages went."

We promised to talk again later.

At 2:30, my intercom buzzer went off.

"Who is it?" I asked.

"Me, of course," came the reply. "I have an appointment with Mr. Maurison at 2:30. How do I get in the door?"

"Push on it when it buzzes," I said, wondering if he was smarter than he sounded.

He may or may not have been smart but he was a smart dresser.

He entered my office fully equipped wearing a dark blue suit with narrow lapels, a full-on red silk tie dangling in front of a long-sleeved white shirt with a light blue collar and gold nugget cufflinks. His shoes looked as if they had been buffed by the world-class bootblack at Grand Central Station and his hair was cut, blow-dried and gelled like the host of a TV reality show.

I wondered why such a classy-looking guy was walking into my office instead of some upper-crust agency on Park Avenue. It wasn't long before I found the answer.

"My name is William," he said. "That's all you need to know. If I hire you, I'll pay you in cash and you won't need to know more that. Do we understand each other?"

I gave a slight nod, trying to look as cool and composed as I could under the circumstances. None of his surreptitious nonsense made any difference to me. After all I'm in this business for the money and as long as my life isn't put in danger or I'm not asked to do something illegal I'll agree with almost anything if it helps move me into a higher tax bracket.

"I'm here because I need to be discreet, off the radar, on the q.t., if you know what I mean. You and your office seem to be about as far off the beaten track as I could find without being so shoddy that I'd have to wear latex gloves for the appointment."

It wasn't the sort of endorsement I'd list in my portfolio but if it was enough of a reason to bring him into my office then it was good enough for me.

"I run a business. It's a good business. I started it from scratch ten years ago when I graduated from college. My father is a wise man. When I asked him for advice, he told me, 'Son, if you want to be a success in life, find something that everybody needs but that nobody wants to do.'

"I gave that a lot of thought and wound up in the porta-potty business. Maybe you've seen my toilets around town. They have the name 'Sweet Stop' on them. It's turned into a big deal. Once I got in bed with the unions I've had more business than I can handle."

So much for his attempt at anonymity.

"Here's the problem. I've been crushing my competition. There's this one outfit called "Royal Throne" that had a virtual lock on the market for years. They got fat and lazy and when I entered the game, I blew them out of the water. They didn't like it and now they're out to get even. They're not trying to compete with me on the business side, they're trying to destroy me . . . and I mean that literally."

"You mean," I asked, "they're putting TNT in your toilets and blowing them up?"

I was trying to be lighthearted but it turned out my question wasn't far off the mark.

"No," William replied, "although they might as well be doing that. All that happens is someone comes along during the night and drills a four-inch hole in the underbelly of my toilets where all the crap goes. It's not dramatic enough to make the news or even the police blotter, but the time and expense it takes to clean up the mess and repair or replace the toilets is cutting my profit margin into confetti. The whole thing stinks."

"What are the police doing about it?"

"They said they'd assign a detective to the case but no one has given me so much as a phone call since. Because I'm a hands-on sort of guy and like to be in control of things I'm not happy when I don't know what's going on. That's why I want to hire a PI— someone who'll be accountable directly to me and only to me. I'm here to see if you're the guy."

"That depends," I said, "on what you want me to do."

"I want you to track the chain of command back to the company leadership and find out who's giving the orders and who's paying the flunkies to cut the holes. If you can find proof then I'll be able to nail them and shut them down with a criminal lawsuit. I know who's doing it but I don't have the evidence. That's what I'm asking you to find . . . the evidence— the smoking gun."

I handed "Sweet Stop" William my boilerplate contract form along with a pen.

"Fill this out," I said, "We can discuss the fine print afterwards."

William said he had hundreds of "Sweet Stop" toilets all over Manhattan but he singled out two construction sites as being the most likely to be hit next. The sabotage strategy appeared to be two-fold:

1. Hit a construction area that had as many union workers on site as possible, and
2. Hit a construction site that was under the most pressure for a completion deadline.

"There were night watchmen on duty at every site I've been attacked," he added, "so I'm assuming they're either incompetent or they've been bought off by someone."

"For whatever it's worth take my advice: Keep at a safe distance and don't get in the way. This is serious business and the Mob could be involved. I don't want you to get hurt. I just want some evidence. Copy?"

"Copy that," I said. "I'll get on the hunt this evening—after I tend to the care and feeding of my wife."

For a dinner menu, I first considered omelets, then frozen TV dinners, then pre-made lasagna from the supermarket. Finally, I decided on waffles with whipped cream, fresh berries and a salad. The salad was to make the meal seem more like dinner than breakfast.

I printed out an online waffle recipe and headed straight up the street to Thor's Pawn Shop.

"Hey, Thor," I said as I walked through the door. "Long time no see. How's Du?"

"Hey Mike. My brother's doing fine, thank you. He's lost 10 pounds and is healthy enough to keep his shop running as usual. What's up with you?"

"Nothing much . . . ."

"Wait a sec," Thor interrupted. "You didn't stop by just to say, 'Hello,' did you. I can tell from the look in your eye."

Thor reads body language and facial expressions like a pro. It's one of the talents that helped him survive the Vietnam War and escape with his brother, his sister-in-law and his aunt after the Americans left everyone behind but themselves.

"You're right as usual," I said. "I wish you could teach me how you do that. In my business, I have to be good at the body language stuff and I'm good enough but I wish I was better.

"I came by to see if Zach was free to help me with a case. I need him tonight if possible."

"Zach's at the apartment with Auntie Nhu. She's older than fossils and not doing very well lately. I'll be home before dark, though, and I can tag-team Zach over to your place by eight o'clock if that's not too late. He's short on cash so I know he'll take the job."

"Good," I said, "and thanks. Give me a call if it doesn't work out."

Zach is Thor's nephew. His parents, Du and Thị Yen own a shop in London just off Trafalgar Square. Du is the one who found the "maybe Rembrandt" painting in a dumpster behind his store. How I came to own it is another story. Zach helps me out as my assistant every so often. He's a good kid and has saved my neck a couple of times. If I had the money I'd hire him full time, but that's another story, too.

At the other end of the street is Juan's corner market where I planned to pick up some lettuce and a tomato along with frozen strawberries and a can of whipped cream.

"*Da nada*," I said as I walked in.

"*Mi pesar*," Juan replied with a smile.

I got the goods and after the exchange of cash, I waved good-by with a "*Buenos dias*."

"*Buenos* tardes," Juan corrected me.

"Thanks, Juan, *auf wienerschnitzel*."

I beat Mona to the apartment by thirty minutes and had the strawberries thawed, the salad tossed and the batter made by the time she walked in.

Mona greeted me with a smile and kiss.

"Welcome home, pilgrim," she said. "Are you planning on staying put for a while, or does the lure of filthy lucre still hold you in its grasp?"

"I'm home until we finish dinner," I replied. "Afterwards, I've got a stakeout lined up with Zach playing the role of Baba Looey. I'll be back late . . . or early. I guess it depends on how you look at it."

"Sounds fun, Mr. McGraw," Mona shot back.

Dinner turned out better than either of us had predicted.

While we were eating, I told her what Connie and I did on our trip, and how we ran into one dead-end after another. When I mentioned the mystery woman with the journal pages, Mona didn't miss a beat.

"Go to the library and ask the Manuscript Librarian if he or she remembers her. You've got a good description and she would have to be registered as a researcher and sign in each time to get into the stacks."

Mona is a librarian at Hunter College, so I knew she was on to something as soon as she said the words, "Go to the library."

Having Mona around sometimes gives me an edge on the other PIs in town. If she was twenty-five years older, she'd be giving Miss Marple and Jessica Fletcher a run for their money, too.

Chapter Seven

The Sound of Buzzing
Monday Evening

After we washed and dried the dishes, I gave Connie a call.

"I never knew you were a researcher," I said.

"There is a lot about me you don't know," Connie replied. "After all, you dropped out of our lives for 12 years, remember?"

So much for the chit-chat.

After I explained what Mona said about a visit to the library I said, "You can do *da kine* the next time you're there; hopefully as soon as possible."

"What?" she replied.

"Just do what Mona said, okay?"

"Okay," she said. "But Mike, you are one weird dude sometimes."

"Mona agrees with you," I said as we hung up on each other.

Two minutes later, my phone rang. It was Connie.

"Why should I go to a library in Central Manhattan when you practically live next door to it?" she said tersely. "Nice try 'Mr. Bait and Switch.' The pea is under your cup. So eat it."

I could tell she was family from the way she talked.

Ever the optimist, I gave it the old university try for a second time.

"Don't get all inflated like a balloon, Connie. You don't have to come all the way into town. You can do the job with a phone call. That's all I'm asking. It'll be piece of pie."

"Eat the pie along with the pea, Mike. *Bon appétit.*"

If Connie had been talking on an old-fashioned dial phone there would have been a loud, audible, "click." Unfortunately, the dramatic effect was completely lost on her smart phone.

Technology always has a caveat attached to it somewhere.

Now that I was the chump who was going to the library, I started sorting through the facts to form a strategy. First off, the mystery woman probably had a day job that tied her up Monday through Friday. Since the manuscript area isn't open on Sundays or

Mondays and closes at 5:30 p.m. during the rest of the week, her library visits would be limited to Saturdays. If I could find a librarian who covered Saturday shifts in the Archives the odds of finding out who the woman was would skyrocket.

The intercom buzzer buzzed. It was Zach, right on time.

"Don't bother coming up," I told him. "I'll be there in a minute."

Mona didn't seem very enthusiastic about my goodnight-goodbye kiss.

"Come back alive if you can," she said.

"I'll give it my best shot," I said, suddenly realizing I had left my Blue Bursa .380 locked away in my office drawer.

Mike's Rule #1 came to mind; the part that goes, "When in danger: Run." It was good advice and I hoped I would take it if I had to.

"What's the job, Boss?" Zach asked as we started walking towards the East River. "I'm all dressed up for a stakeout. Is it outside or inside this time?"

"Outside," I answered, "and I fixed a thermos with enough coffee for both of us."

Some big-time investor was building a massive parking garage twelve blocks south and east from my office. The site was on Williams's shortlist of places ripe for the picking. It was closer than any of the others so it made sense to case it out first. Besides, I had walked past it recently and not only knew where the toilets were but also knew a good place to squat while we kept our eyes on them.

There was a row of four toilets lined up on the construction side of an eight-foot cyclone fence. The fence was wrapped in a dust cover, but fortunately for us, the toilets were next to the truck entrance so we had a clear view of the "Sweet Stops" through the undraped gate.

The night watchman came by the toilets at the top of the hour and then every ten minutes after. Except for the intermittent street traffic, he was the only entertainment we had until a few minutes before 1:00 a.m. when a man hopped out of the passenger side of a pickup. There wasn't anything written on the side of the truck but I did jot down the numbers and letters on the plate.

The man made his way to the gate, pulled a key out of his pocket, unlocked the gate and let himself in. Coincidently, the night watchman happened to miss both his top-of-the-hour visit and the one after that.

The sound of buzzing could be heard four separate times, and in less than ten minutes, the man was back on the street with the gate locked behind him. As he stood waiting for the truck, I added a dozen telephoto portraits to go along with the video I had already taken of him "open sesame-ing" his way through the gate.

When the truck arrived, I snapped some rapid-fire pics of the front window, but since the headlights were pointed in my direction, I didn't think the photos were going to tell me much about the guy who was driving.

I immediately texted William: "fyi upper east side parking garage hit have lead on suspect good progress more later."

"That was lucky," I said as we started our way back. "Five hours and the work is done."

"That's five and a *half* hours," Zach said, "at $15 an hour. You own me eighty-two bucks plus change. I should add combat pay but you brought coffee so we're even."

"Thanks, Zach," I said as we parted ways. "I'll give you a call the next time I face a long night hiding behind a dumpster in a dark alley in a bad neighborhood."

"Thanks, Mike. You're a pal."

Chapter Eight

Black Sonja
Tuesday Morning

I slept in. When I woke up, Mona had already left for work. There was a note inviting me to join her for lunch. I texted her, *"c u at noon neil's."*

After eating a toasted bagel, I wrote up a first-draft report on the night's work and called a friend in the NYPD asking him to run a check on the license number on the truck. The owner turned out to be someone named Leslie McGillicutty who lived in Queens. His record was clean.

The next step took a few clicks on my computer. There I came across the only Leslie McGillicutty in the whole of New York State and he happened to live in Queens. His name also popped up in a local news article that mentioned him as an assistant manager of a girl's softball team.

A family guy, I thought to myself as I Google-mapped his address and began figuring out how best to blend in with his shadow.

With that task under wraps, I sauntered over to Lexington and caught the train south to the New York Central Library.

The librarian in the Manuscripts section turned out to be a person named Sara. When I described the mystery woman, she looked through the "check-in-check-out" records but couldn't find any name associated with the journal in question.

"Talk to Mark," she said. "Mark Robertson. He's working the front desk this morning. He usually works weekends and sometimes fills in up here. Good luck to you. I hope you find her. If she damaged one of our books we need to hold her accountable and, if we're lucky, get the pages back."

"I'll drag her straight over, but only after she spends a day or two in a pillory on Times Square."

Mark turned out to be more helpful than I could have possibly hoped. After I showed him my PI badge and filled him in on the details, he looked like a cat, tensing to spring from someone's lap.

"Let's see . . . a young woman with short, black hair and wearing a leather motorcycle outfit . . . hmm . . . there can't be too many of those hanging around that section of the library so it's got to be Sonja."

"Sonja?" I echoed.

"Yeah, Sonja. Like *Red Sonja* in the comics, except the comic book Sonja has long red hair and doesn't wear very much . . . ."

I cut him off in mid sentence.

"I know who Red Sonja is. She's the 'Warrior Woman of Hysterectomy' or something like that. It's been a long time since I . . .but who cares. What matters is who *Black* Sonja is and how do I find her."

"I'm sorry, Mr. . . uh . . . ."

"Maurison," I said as I handed him my card.

"I'm sorry, Mr. Maurison, but our patron's personal information is confidential. I can't tell you anything, but if you want, you can look over my shoulder when I bring her name up on the computer."

That, I suppose, is why they call them public servants.

"Sonja Ingersoll" it said, alongside a phone number and an address in Queens—a bit of information that confirmed the restaurant manager's guess about her accent. The thought that Sonja and Leslie McGillicutty might be neighbors flickered through my consciousness for a millisecond until I redirected the neural stimulation to a different section of my brain.

"Thanks, Mark. You've been a big help. If I find Sonja I'll try to get the journal pages back where they belong."

"My pleasure," he said, "and don't forget: 'A book a day keeps the mind at play!'"

I made a mental note to pass that one on to Mona.

Finding folks is what I do for a living, so tracking down Sonja-of-Queens was going to be a lot easier than finding Private Ryan. As it turned out, the name "Sonja Ingersoll" was as rare as McGillicutty's, but the Sonja who lived in Queens popped up all over the internet. She taught history at a high school in Brooklyn and was a candidate for a PhD in History at CUNY-Queens; the same school where Mona was one semester away from earning her Masters Degree in Library Science.

I guessed Sonja's thesis probably had something to do with the French and Indian War. Why else would she have been browsing through a Colonial soldier's journal from 1755?

The plot was thickening faster than hair on a Chia Pet and unless Connie and I did something soon, the path to a happy ending was going to be as impenetrable as concrete.

"Connie," I said after punching her number into my phone. "Now is the time for all good men to come to the aid of their country."

She immediately replied, "The quick brown fox jumps over the lazy dog."

Right then and there, I knew that with a daughter like Connie there must be more to Aunt Lucille than I had been willing to concede.

"'Now is the time,'" I repeated. "'The iron is hot and in the fire.'"

"You sound like a union boss declaring it's time to strike," Connie teased back.

"Seriously," I said, trying to restore some measure of sanity to the conversation, "the mystery woman is named Sonja Ingersoll . . . ."

After bringing Connie up to speed I asked, "Do you want me to make a visit to Queens by myself or do you want to meet and go together?"

"Together," she said. "I'd hate to miss out on the *denouement*."

That was when I remembered Connie had majored in French, apparently with a minor in Poirot.

"Are you still on vacation?" I asked.

"All week; so just say 'When and Where' and I'll be there."

"Pack a bag in case we need to leave town again. Meet me in front of the Jamaica Station around Noon. I'll give you a call fifteen minutes before I get there."

While I was on the train, I phoned Zach and asked him to try to dig up more info on McGillicutty.

Next, I texted Mona to tell her I was cancelling lunch . . . and dinner. At the end of the message I left a long line of question marks to cover whatever contingencies showed up. Even though Mona is used to my schedule shifting as quickly as a Formula One driver I knew she wasn't going to be happy when she discovered our date was trumped by my rendezvous with Connie.

Chapter Nine

Baba Looey
Tuesday Afternoon

As we were driving into Queens, I asked Connie to take me past Les McGillicutty's address. It was a modest two-story, traditional neighborhood house with a small front yard and not much else to distinguish it from the other houses on the block. The same pickup truck I had seen the night before was parked on the street out front. It was tempting to stop and snoop around but I owed it to Connie to keep Sonja in the spotlight at least through Act One.

Sonja's place also turned out to be a house. I didn't know whether she was married, single, rich or poor, but the fact she was living in a house instead of an apartment meant either she was able to afford it or she was renting with roommates.

I was wrong on both counts.

The lady who answered the door turned out to be Sonja's mother.

Like so many other young adults working full-time jobs while trying to pay off student loans, Sonja was still living with a parent.

"No," her mother said when we asked if Sonja was home. "She's back at work today. Who should I say called?"

I shot a look at Connie but before I could think of an answer Connie said, "Two colleagues who share her interest in quarries."

I started to hand over my business card as a contact but Connie grabbed my hand and whispered that having a private eye stop by the house might not leave a good first-impression.

"Here," Connie said as she scribbled on a piece of scratch paper. "This is my email address and phone number. Like it says, my name is Connie and I'd love to meet your daughter. We have so much in common."

We felt like Lewis and Clark must have felt when they took to the river in St. Louis on the start of their trek to the Pacific. We had made a start with Sonja but what was coming next we had no idea.

Connie and I had hardly pulled away from the curb in front of Sonja's house when Zach called me back.

"Hey, Mike," he said. "I looked up 'Royal Throne' and gave them a call. When I got past the recorded message, I asked to speak with Les McGillicutty. The receptionist said, 'Oh, you must mean Leslie. Leslie doesn't work here anymore, but still comes by every now and then to say hello. I'm sorry I can't be of more help.'

"That's the scoop," Zach said as his sentence ground to a stop. "I thought you'd like to know."

"Sounds like another piece of the pie," I said, as an image of pie was quickly associated with a pea under a cup, which morphed into a princess lying on a stack of mattresses. "Thanks for the good work, Zach. Du would be proud. Now keep at it and see what else you can scrape up."

I was going to add a closing thought but my phone went as dead as road kill.

"Connie, can I use your car charger?"

"Sure, go ahead. It'll work if you have an iphone.

With an Android in my hand, I was out of luck.

"What do we do now?" Connie said.

"If you have the time let's go over to McGillicutty's place. If he goes and comes with the truck we can follow him. If he doesn't show up we can go back and try to catch Sonja when she gets home from school. You can be my Baba Looey."

Connie pulled the car to the side of the street so she could stare at me straight in the face.

"Mike," she reprised, "'sometimes you are one weird dude,' and this, by the way, is one of those times. What do you mean, 'Baba Looey?'"

"Nothing," I said, realizing I had slipped into the delusion that Connie and Mona were clones of each other. "I'm just saying that you can be Zach for a few hours if you're up for it."

"Zach?" she said, still staring me in the face. "Who the hell is Zach?"

"He was at my wedding and the reception and he's Thor's nephew . . . and that doesn't mean anything to you either, does it?"

"It's okay, Mike," Connie cut in. "It doesn't matter how Baba Looney you are. I like you this way and I'm glad you're my cousin. If you want me to be Zach for a few hours then call me Zach."

She smiled a smile that for one transcendent moment transformed her face into the face of my mother. The vision jolted me into the realization that Mom was just about Connie's age when she evaporated into thin air. It was the same face and the same smile I later projected onto the central figure of Picasso's *Demoiselles D'Avignon*, a painting that hangs in the Fifth Floor Gallery of the Museum of Modern Art. Talking to Mom at the MoMA has been an important part of my life ever since, but seeing her smile on the face of a real person threw me for a fastball.

I wondered why I had never seen my mother's face in her sister Lucille . . . but that was probably because from my perspective, Aunt Lucille had always been older than my mother ever lived to be.

As I reentered reality, I noticed Connie had turned her head away and was pulling back into traffic. My mother's smile, however, was still on her face and I was surprised to realize that, until that moment, I had never noticed how beautiful my cousin was . . . beautiful . . . like my mother.

Soon we had parked within sight of McGillicutty's house and had begun munching drive-thru fries we picked up along the way. We had just started in on the burgers when the spitting image of a young Rosie O'Donnell on steroids came out of the house, got into the truck and started driving down the street with her tailpipe pointed at us like a small canon.

"Well?" Connie asked. "Are we going to follow her or wait for Les?"

"Whoever she is, she's the one in the truck so we might as well see where she's going."

We followed her straight to Manhattan, across the Queensboro Bridge and onto the Upper East Side. When she came to the construction site where Zach and I spent the previous night, she downshifted into slow motion like a low-rider cruising a small town Main Street at 9:00 p.m. on a Saturday night.

In full view of the "Sweet Stop" toilets she pulled up to the truck gate, got out of the truck and handed a white, letter-sized envelope through the fence by some guy in a hard hat. After a ten-minute drive south along the East River she turned the truck into a fenced area filled with portable toilets. The toilets had the words "Royal Throne" painted on them featuring a red and gold crown hovering over the letter "R."

"You know what?" I said to no one in particular although Connie happened to be within earshot. "I think we found our man."

"You're getting weird again," Connie said under her breath.

Ignoring her comment, I continued, but this time talking to her on purpose.

"We thought he was a he, but he's a she. I don't think I told you this, but I couldn't see the face of the person driving the truck last night. Later, when I found out who owned it, I figured that Les McGillicutty had been the driver and I was right, but his full name is Leslie and this particular Leslie happens to be more like Leslie Caron than Leslie Nielson."

If I had been Perry Mason, this would have created the dramatic moment when Hamilton Burger stands up and shouts, "Objection, your Honor!"

It may not have been the *denouement* Connie had been expecting that afternoon, but it made me feel giddy to have figured out who dunnit . . . I don't, of course, mean "giddy" in the sense that giving

Mona a flower makes me feel giddy, but . . . well . . . you get the idea.

I don't suppose it was a home run, either, but at least we had gotten someone on base. Sometime soon, we were going to have a chance to bat again and, with luck, bring the runner to the plate.

I looked at my watch and turned to Connie.

"It's only 2:15 p.m. Since you have to drive home anyway I'll go with you and we can swing by and see if Sonja's back from school. Afterwards you can drop me off at Jamaica and I'll catch the train back to Manhattan."

When we pulled onto Sonja's street at 2:45 p.m. there was a black Honda motorcycle sitting the driveway.

"Pull in and block it," I said.

As we stopped, a young woman with short black hair, completely cocooned in black leather came out of the house and headed for the Honda.

"Hello!" Connie shouted as she stepped out of the car with a friendly smile. "You must be Sonja."

Sonja met Connie face-to-face half-way to the bike.

"Take my advice," Sonja said with an intensity that chilled me. "Stop looking for quarries. They can be very dangerous and I would hate to see you . . . " her eyes turned to look at me . . . "either of you get hurt. Give it up and go home. With luck I'll never see you again."

She walked over to the bike, pulled on her helmet, sat down, cranked it up, and blew past us leaving behind a small cloud of exhaust and burnt rubber as a memento.

"Just because she doesn't want to see us again," Connie said as we scrambled back into the car, "doesn't mean we can't see *her* again!"

Connie left a small memento of her own as we sped down the street to see Sonja again.

It turned out Sonja was one of the safest and most cautious bikers on the East Coast. She kept to the speed limit, never passed cars along the shoulder or between lanes and always signaled a right or left turn in advance. In other words, following her from a safe distance was a breeze . . . until we came to Hartford.

I had just texted Mona on Connie's phone, telling her not to expect me home for dinner or breakfast when Sonja turned Interstate 91 into the Daytona Speedway. As Connie's subcompact hit 85 mph something under the hood said, "Excuse me while I take a siesta." As we coasted off the freeway, we saw Sonja hit warp speed and disappear into interstellar space.

Connie's investment in Triple-A paid off when the tow truck arrived within ten minutes and hauled us to the nearest dealer Service Center. Connie's car was still under warranty and whatever it took to save a few bucks for repairs was worth the extra five miles it took to get there.

"I wonder if they have loaners?" Connie mused out loud.

As we sat, waiting to hear whether the siesta was terminal or not I plugged my phone into a wall socket for a recharge. Less than a minute later, while Connie was tapping what seemed to be the opening chapter of Moby Dick into her phone, the sound of Ravel came wafting out of my re-energized Android. It was Mona.

"Mike," she said. I got your text but I've been phoning and leaving you messages for hours. Where are you and what's going on?"

She didn't wait for an answer.

"Mike, the reason I've been trying to reach you is because the National Gallery in London has been calling all afternoon. They finally gave up on you and called me instead. The research team finished its evaluation of Du's painting and decided it's a real Rembrandt—fake signature and all! Isn't that exciting?"

"No kidding!" I said. "That's great news!"

In one sense, the news *was* exciting but, in another sense it was not much of a surprise. This was mostly because Grandpa van Rijn, the Rembrandt *Self Portrait* hanging on the wall of the Metropolitan Museum of Art, had already told us it had been one of his favorite paintings and one he had never signed. Just like Mom at the MoMA, I have family and friends hanging on the walls of most of the major museums in NYC and some of them, like Grandpa, can be quite chatty at times.

"Now what happens?" I asked Mona.

"Since there's no provenance for it and since it seems to have been stolen from somewhere they are going to return it to the National Gallery and keep it on ice for the time being. Interpol hasn't found any connection to a recent theft, so they're pursuing the possibility it was stolen from a Jewish estate by the Nazis. It could take years to decide whether it's ours to keep or not. I've already phoned Thor to pass the news on to Zach and Du."

"Mona," I asked with a hint of misplaced curiosity, "you've done all this while clocking time within the sacred silence of Hunter Library?"

"Yes," came the terse and somewhat uninspired answer.

"So," she continued without taking a breath, "when are you coming home this time?"

"At the moment it's not a matter of *when* but a matter of *how*," I explained.

After talking through the situation, the options became clear. Connie's car could be fixed and ready to go in an hour or two; we could borrow a loaner; we could rent another car; we could take the train or bus back to Manhattan or Mona could drive my friend Sid's car up to Hartford and pick us up later in the evening.

"There's one other option," Connie said, pointing through the Service Center window as a red Miata pulled up to the curb.

Joe and Connie wrapped each other in a brief imitation of an unconsummated corporate merger and walked back to include me in the conversation.

"Sorry," Joe said without offering his hand for a shake, "Miatas don't have back seats. There's only room for two."

With the choice of passengers limited to either Connie or me, my guts announced I had already been given the short straw and was going to have to either walk or call Mona for a ride home.

To no one's surprise, my guts were right.

As we talked, Connie's eyes stayed locked on Joe's as if they were Siamese Twins.

Eventually, however, Connie surgically separated herself and turned towards me.

"Then it's settled," she announced in the same tone of divine rightness she had used the day before. "Mike will stay here until my car is ready to drive. Hopefully, that will only be an hour or two. I turned the key in with the car."

When she had finished pontificating, I asked as discretely as I could, "And what the hell are you two going to be doing while I have the distinct honor of sitting here on my butt, surrounded by the smell of gasoline, cheap coffee and stale popcorn?"

"I don't know," Joe replied prosaically. "Maybe you could read a newspaper and do the crossword."

They then reprised their disappearing act in the Miata.

Insofar as Connie was unstable, randomly compulsive and adept at disappearing without a moment's notice she was starting to look more and more like my mother every minute.

Five minutes after they left, a mechanic came over to tell me Connie's transmission was DOA and it would be at least three days before they could get a rebuilt replacement into the shop. The good news was the drive train was still under warranty and the transmission wouldn't cost Connie a dime. I would have felt happy for Connie except for the fact I was so angry at her I could have bitten a spark plug in half.

I was even angrier when the mechanic told me it was 6:10 p.m. and the service department had closed at 6:00.

"Hey," I said as he was walking away. "Do you mind if I get my bag out of the car before you go?"

"Sure," he said. "But hurry up. It's been a long day and I want to go home."

"Me, too," I whispered to myself.

Chapter Ten

Detour

Tuesday Evening

Auto joints are not usually located in the best neighborhoods. They are, in fact, not usually located in neighborhoods of any kind. They usually sit on property that would have been a vacant lot if someone hadn't built a dealership on it.

Maybe I'm exaggerating but I don't think any suburban resident has ever said to his wife during breakfast, "Honey, let's walk over to the car dealership after we've cleaned up the dishes."

This is because the nearest car dealership is never within walking distance of anything. The dealership in Hartford that was attempting to resuscitate the corpse of Connie's car was no exception to this rule. Fortunately, however, the lady at the sales desk was kind enough to call a cab to pick me up and take me somewhere . . . anywhere that wasn't an auto joint . . . preferably someplace with a menu.

After three minutes on the meter, the cabbie dropped me in front of a small building that looked like what a diner would look like if designed by a movie studio in Burbank. Although I had never seen this particular make and model before I had no doubt there were at least several dozen clones scattered around the North East like spilled beans. There was probably a map showing where each franchise was located printed on the flimsy paper place mats that outfits like this put on the food trays.

I ordered a prime rib French dip sandwich with a side salad and fries.

The *au juice* was wet enough but the meat was as dry as leather along the edges. As a bonus, what the menu called a "Ciabatta Roll" was so hard that an eighteen-wheeler would have damaged its tires if it had run over it.

I was so hungry I ate it all anyway, and then washed it down with root beer from a dispenser that had run out of CO_2. My life flashed in front of my eyes and all I could see was a big-city loser standing in the dark next to an Interstate on-ramp with his thumb held up in the air like a surrender flag.

My phone started playing *Bolero* again and I decided it was time to change the ring tone to something more contemporary like Stravinsky.

It turned out to be Mona checking in to see if Connie and I were still stranded.

"One of us is," I said.

"Which one?" Mona asked.

"Me," I said.

I added a small sob and a sniffle for emphasis.

"Poor baby, "Mona emoted badly. "Sid's using his car tonight so if you're stuck I can't help you. But I called Robert and he said he'd be willing to drive Chia's car up to Hartford this evening and bring you home trussed up like a dead deer on the front bumper of the car."

"I'll take Robert," I said with a sigh of relief, "and Connie can go to . . . to . . . she can go to Joe for all I care.

"Mona," I cried. "Get me out of here!"

Robert arrived at 9:00 p.m.

I had drunk so much coffee I had to go to the Men's Room one more time before I felt safe enough to climb into the car.

"Home, James," I said with yawn.

Robert is my best friend. He was the Best Man at my wedding two months after I was the Best Man at his. He is the security guard at the front entrance to the Museum of Modern Art where I go to see my Mom. He is also the nicest person I have ever known.

"The gas is on me," I offered.

"Then I won't light a match until you wash it off," Robert said.

Robert doesn't say much but when he does say something it's usually not quite what you expected.

"Mike," he asked, "why are you in Hartford?"

"Because I'm an idiot," I answered.

"I don't get it," he said. "Why did you have to go all the way to Hartford to be an idiot? You could have been just as much of an idiot if you had stayed home."

The logic was airtight.

"Let's go to Albany," I said.

I was surprised to hear myself say it because until that moment I hadn't even thought about driving to Albany.

"Why do you want to go to Albany?" Robert asked.

"I don't know," I said. "I really don't know."

"That's good enough for me," Robert said as he reversed direction at the next interchange and started driving north towards Springfield.

I can't say the drive from Hartford to Albany was anything special. The reason I can't say it is because when we drove it was dark and I couldn't tell if it was special or not.

Robert and I kept each other awake by telling stories about our honeymoons. Robert and Chia went to visit Chia's grandmother in Puerto Rico and Mona and I went to London, Paris, Florence and

Rome where we were supposed to have a good time but wound up with three kidnappings, one heart attack, two art thefts and a Rembrandt *Self Portrait* with my name on the pink slip.

Robert got to go to the beach.

I also had time to fill Robert in on the collapsed tunnel in Albany, the journal with the pages missing, the "bried gld," the quary, the French River and Sonja. It took so long to explain it all that it was Midnight in Albany before I finished.

"Now what?" Robert asked.

That particular question had been asked so many times during the past three days it was in danger of replacing, "Are we there yet?" as the most annoying road trip question of all time.

"That's a good question," I said. "Let's find a bed and I'll sleep on it."

Robert was awake enough to laugh at my repartee but I was too tired to realize I had said something funny.

That night I dreamed about worms.

Chapter Eleven

Worms
Wednesday Morning

Robert snores. I had never known that before.

Fortunately, he only snores when he is asleep. Otherwise, driving long distances with him would be very annoying.

But back to the worms.

The worms I dreamed about looked like squiggly lines; lines that were trying to tell me something. They weren't talking out loud or anything but they seemed to be playing some earthy version of charades—with the distinct disadvantage of not having any arms, legs or faces to help get the words across. Another communication handicap might have been that their vocabulary was limited to describing the four thousand varieties of dirt found in New England. For whatever reason, I couldn't figure out what they were trying to tell me.

Since I wasn't getting anywhere with the worms I walked over to Robert's bed and tried to shake him awake.

"Robert," I said quietly. "It's 7:30 in the morning. I'm wide awake and I'm hungry."

Nothing happened.

"Robert," I said loudly enough to be heard in the adjoining room. "Wake up or I'll call you 'Bob.'"

There are only a few things that Robert doesn't like and one of them is being called 'Bob.' So of course, he immediately sat up in bed, wide-awake and ready to start the day.

"Shouldn't you phone the museum to tell them you're not coming in this morning?" I asked.

"No," Robert replied. "If I had to work today I might have driven to Hartford to bring you home but I wouldn't have driven to Albany. After all, I'm not the idiot—you are."

Once again, the logic was airtight.

At breakfast, I grabbed a small box of crayons and one of the children's menus that restaurants use to keep small kids happy while their parents inhale their breakfast during the three minutes the little darlings aren't screaming for attention. In other words, as far as parents are concerned the menus and crayons are worth their weight in gold.

Speaking of gold, I took one of the crayons and tried to draw Robert a copy of the journal map.

When I was finished, Robert took one look at it and said, "That looks like a worm."

He was right. The squiggly line Connie and I thought was either an arrow or the French River had suddenly turned into the worm of my dreams.

"It doesn't look like a river," Robert said. "It doesn't look like an arrow, either."

"Okay, then," I probed. "What does it look like to you . . . besides a worm?"

Robert nibbled on his English muffin while he thought about the question.

"It looks like . . ." he hesitated for a moment. "It looks like a tunnel . . . maybe like a drawing of the tunnel the person wrote about in the journal. Or maybe it's a different tunnel, but you asked and that's the best answer I can think of."

"That would mean," I thought out loud, "that the ✠ is marking a spot in or around the tunnel."

"Robert," I said without thinking out loud, "You're a genius. Now all we have to do is see if the shape of the tunnel matches the shape of the squiggly line in the journal."

"If opposites attract," Robert said, "and I'm a genius, then that would make you . . . ."

"Oh, shut up," I said, "or I won't pay for your breakfast."

There were three messages left on my phone during the night. One was from Connie wondering where I was, one was from Mona wondering where I was and one was from a client who said he thought he had an appointment with me yesterday afternoon and was wondering where I was.

First, I texted Connie that I was in Albany. Second, I texted Mona that I was in Albany with Robert, and third, I left a message on my client's phone explaining I had been called out of town on an emergency and wasn't able to cancel his appointment because I didn't take his phone number with me.

Mikes Survival Rule #3: "If you're caught in a corner, tell a lie—the bigger the better."

Checkout wasn't until 11:00 a.m. but since neither of us had any luggage we checked out early and headed in the direction of Schenectady. With the help of my phone's GPS we found my cousin Ben's house. It was exactly as Connie said, one block away from the sinkhole.

Although the tunnel had collapsed two months earlier, the city, county and state were still arguing over what to do about it. In the meantime, the street repair guys had created a clever way to shore things up with old railroad ties and concrete lane dividers. They then trimmed the four-lane road down to two lanes so traffic could keep moving without having someone with a flag make things worse than they already were.

A temporary cyclone fence had been set up to keep drunks and people like me from falling into the hole. Looking down I could see where the tunnel was still intact and heading off in both directions from the point of collapse.

One direction pointed toward a second cyclone fence that had been set up in a vacant lot. This, I assumed was where the entrance to the tunnel had been found under an otherwise functionless manhole cover.

The other half of the tunnel pointed in the opposite direction where it had led the road repair crew to a dead end and a pile of cocaine.

Robert and I paced the length of the tunnel and came up with 110 feet plus or minus an ankle. It was hard to guess how the tunnel squiggled its way under the ground from one place to another but using our imaginations we came up with a line that matched the first half of the journal drawing exactly. Curiously, it was the half of the line that did not include the ✠.

"What do you think, Robert? I asked.

"I think the lines match. At least the part of the tunnel we walked over. But the line on the map is twice as long."

The conclusion was obvious.

If the line drawn in the journal was a map of this particular tunnel, then the tunnel didn't originally end where it did now but went at least another 90 feet beyond the dead end. That section of the tunnel must have caved-in and been cut it in half years ago. Or maybe someone sealed it off on purpose, maybe to hide whatever was in there.

"Like 'bried gld?'" Robert suggested.

"Yeah," I said. "Like that."

We walked over and stood above the spot where the tunnel dead-ended.

"Maybe there's another man-hole cover over there," Robert suggested as he pointed beyond where the tunnel had come to an end.

From where we stood, the road veered south so, if the tunnel continued as it appeared to do on the map, the other end would be underneath the adjacent vacant lot. This lot was not as vacant as the other one. There were at least a dozen maples and an equal number of thick tangled clumps of blackberry bushes covering most of it. Finding a tunnel entrance did not look promising.

While I was wandering through the bushes staring at my feet, Robert came over and said, "I'll be darned. Look over there."

He was pointing towards a small open area at the far end of the lot. I could see a motorcycle leaning against a tree. It was a Honda.

The motorcycle had New York plates and when I ran a check on them via my friend at the NYPD they turned out to be registered to Sonja. But where was Sonja?

The engine was cold and there was a thin coating of dust on the gas tank indicating it had been sitting there for a while. It didn't make sense that Sonja would park her expensive investment in the middle of a vacant lot and then walk away, leaving it unlocked and visible from several places along the street.

Even so, considering how close we were to the main road the spot where we were standing was remarkably secluded. Trash and beer bottles were scattered everywhere; evidence that the site morphed into Party Central as soon as the sun went down on Friday nights.

"Can I help you?"

The voice was deep, resonant and clearly did not belong to Sonja. When we turned around, we saw a man wearing jeans and an olive colored polo shirt. His tanned, handsome, middle-aged face was adorned with an almost-convincing imitation of a friendly smile.

"Nice bike," I said.

"Yes, it is," he replied.

"Is it yours?" I asked.

"Yes," he said.

It was obvious I wasn't the only person with a Rule #3.

"We heard about the tunnel and thought we'd stop by to take a look at it," I said, willing to take a lie-detector test to prove it.

"The tunnel is over there," the man pointed. "Why are you over here?"

Robert, God bless him, came to the rescue.

"I had to take a pee," he said.

"Oh," the man said, sounding relieved. "Then I guess you don't need my help."

He walked away and so did we.

"Who was that?" Robert asked.

"I don't know but something is afoot . . . or amiss . . . or . . . out of joint . . . or some other literary cliché I can't put my finger on at the moment. In any case, the guy's guarding the place and my guess is he knows where Sonja is, too, which reminds me of another cliché."

"What's that?" Robert asked.

"'I have a bad feeling about this,'" I said, as we looked both ways before crossing the street.

"This looks like a good spot," I said when we had gotten to the other side, across from the tunnel collapse.

"Why is this a good spot?" Robert asked. "It a sidewalk."

"Because we get a clear view of Sonja's bike, that's why."

After twenty minutes Robert said, "Uh, Mike? Why are we here? I'm supposed to be running errands around town today."

"Because . . . " I answered " . . . because Mona says I'm obsessive compulsive."

"I already know that," Robert said. "But what's that got to do with sitting on a sidewalk across from a sinkhole in Albany?"

"Curiosity, I guess. Or maybe it's the gold. I'm not sure. But it probably isn't the gold. I mean that's part of it, but I just want to figure things out. It's like a puzzle . . . like one of those jigsaw puzzles where they don't have the picture on the box and you've got to put the pieces together one at a time until . . . ."

I paused to rethink what I was saying.

"Robert, to answer your question, I guess I just want to see what the picture looks like."

Five minutes later Robert said, "Oh."

Then he added, "I'm going to get the car and park it here. I'd rather be sitting in a car than on concrete."

A few minutes later, he was back with the car. Robert was right. It was more comfortable than the sidewalk and we could still see Sonja's bike in the distance.

"The car is a good idea anyway," I said, "because we'll be able to follow the motorcycle if it goes anywhere."

Chapter Twelve

Missing in Action
Wednesday Afternoon

At 11:30 a.m. my guts started complaining about the lack of food.

I usually do what my guts tell me and they were telling me to buy something to eat right now.

"Robert," I said, "stay in the car. I'm going to walk over and buy a burger combo. What do you want me to get for you?"

"I'll have the Norwegian Anchovy Salad with Walrus blubber dressing on the side."

I waited patiently through the mandatory pause and drumroll.

"If they're out I'll have two Kiddie Kombos and a diet root beer."

It was lame, even for Robert.

"I'll be right back."

When I came back with the food Robert and the car were gone and I was lurched again.

My phone beeped with an incoming text message. It was from Robert and it looked as if it had been typed while driving which is not, of course, a good idea under any circumstances.

Except maybe this one.

"*Loaded bik on trk blu frd 8950 fg twrds schehedhjgfy*"

I understood what he was trying to say without any trouble at all . . . because I don't know how to spell Schenectady either.

The license plate ID was missing a number but none of that mattered because the fries were getting cold and there wasn't a car for me to sit in. I backtracked to the burger joint and ate Robert's Kiddie meals before I started in on my own. I don't like diet soda.

I was getting a refill on my cola when my phone beeped again.

"*stoppt at speedy car rentl going to chek somethbng bye*"

Robert obviously hadn't activated the auto-spell option on his phone.

I texted back: "*I enjoyed your lunch mine was good too*"

Robert didn't text back.

After waiting fifteen minutes, I called a cab and told the driver to take me to the nearest Speedy Car

Rental. Seven minutes and twenty dollars later we were there. Robert's car was there too, parked in the shade of a tree.

I sauntered over to the office to check the place out.

"Got any used rentals for sale?" I asked.

"We don't sell them to the public," said the middle-aged man with a two-foot long grey and red beard and fingernails that looked as if they had been scraping carbon paper all morning.

When I looked over his shoulder, I could see a blue Ford pickup parked in the garage. The truck's bed was empty and there was no sign of anyone else except Redbeard and me.

"Okay, thanks," I said. "By the way, do you have a Men's Room I could use?"

"Sure," he said. "Right through there and to the left."

I followed his directions into the garage and immediately saw Sonja's motorcycle in the back corner partly covered by an oily drop cloth. I walked into the restroom, counted to ten, flushed the toilet and came back into the garage.

The license number on the truck matched Robert's text perfectly except now I had the missing number.

"Thanks," I said as I walked outside and headed back towards the street.

When I was out of sight of the office window, I made a right turn and walked around the back of the garage. There were six or seven parked cars but nothing that helped me figure out what had happened to Robert.

Next I walked around and over to Robert's car. It was unlocked and for some reason he had left the keys sitting on the seat. Apparently, he planned to be away from the car for only a few minutes at the most. But why didn't he come back? And where was he now?

I sat in the car and pulled out my phone to call Mona. I noticed there was a text message from Robert I had somehow missed. It was sent three minutes after he texted me about Speedy Rental.

"vacnt lot guy hre but no Sonj"

That was it. That was all. There was nothing for me to do except file a missing person report on Robert. But even that would be a waste of time because the police wouldn't give it a second thought until a day or two had gone past. After all, Robert was an adult and I had no evidence he was in trouble.

I couldn't tell the police about Sonja, either, because she was none of my business and I didn't have any evidence she was missing or in trouble, either.

That's why I called Mona.

"Mona," I said. "This is Mike."

"I know," Mona said. "Your name is staring at me from my phone. How's the prospecting going?"

"Mona," I started over, "things aren't going well at all. Robert is missing. I'm sitting in his car but there's no Robert. I think he might have been kidnapped because of something that has to do about the tunnel and I know the police aren't going to do anything for a couple of days so I need some help. I'm really worried and I need you to come up right away . . . you and Chia, too. See if you can get Sid's car or rent one but just get up here as fast as you can—this afternoon. Please!"

"Is this a joke?" Mona asked. "Tell me it's a joke. It's a joke, right? Mike?"

"No joke, Mona," I said. "Give me a call every thirty minutes and tell me where you are. When you get close to Albany, I'll tell you where we'll meet. Got it?"

"Mike," Mona shouted into the phone, which was not a good thing since she was probably at work somewhere in the library. "What the hell have you done with Robert! What is wrong with you!"

"Mona," I said. "Robert already knows I'm an idiot. So just call Chia and get yourself up here now! Quit your job if you have to. But . . . ."

Mona cut me off.

"Mike, I feel like the U.S. Cavalry officer must have felt; the one who was sent to find out why

Custer and his men were late coming back to the fort for dinner. Don't do anything until I get there."

"Call Chia," I repeated, but Mona had already ended the call.

Part of me wanted to start looking for Robert and Sonja immediately, but the rest of me wanted to stay put until Mona and Chia got here. It was a few minutes past 1:00 in the afternoon and the girls wouldn't be here until after 4:00. I had three hours to kill but I didn't want to do something that would cause me to disappear before they came to the rescue. I may be an idiot but I'm not a fool.

Since I didn't know what else to do I drove back to Bargain Burgers and sat down as per Mike's Survival Rule #2.

As soon as I got there, I phoned Connie.

"What are you doing in Albany without me!" she shouted into the phone before I could say "Hello."

"Because you took off with Joe and left me without a car and without a clue as to when or if I'd ever see you again. I was hungry and I needed a place to spend the night and you weren't being any help at all . . . ."

"Okay, Mike," Connie said. "I know I blew it. I'm sorry. But what's the deal with Albany?"

Connie listened while I told her about Robert, the tunnel, the vacant lot guy, and the Speedy Rental Car Company. Next, I told her about the car I was sitting in and I told her about telling Mona and Chia to join me in Albany, pronto.

"Mike," she said. "My car won't be ready until Friday at the earliest and maybe not until Monday afternoon. I want to be in Albany, too. I thought we were partners . . . together . . . on a treasure hunt . . . like a team . . . ."

"If you want to get to Albany, you can take a bus, or take a cab if you're lucky enough to win the lottery. You know I'm not very happy about you . . . what you did . . . twice . . . with Joe."

"You're right, Mike. I guess the only way I can make it up to you and make Joe pay for causing all this trouble is to have him drive me to Albany this afternoon. We'll see you in a couple of hours. Bye."

"Connie!" I shouted, loudly enough to cause everyone in the burger place to either start staring at me or start sucking on their straws out of embarrassment. "Don't come up here with Joe!"

I yelled out the name "Connie" one more time but it was no use. Connie, just like everyone else I had talked to on the phone lately, had hung up before I was finished talking.

I felt the urge to eat comfort food. For me that usually means pizza but finding pizza in a burger place is like trying to find escargot in a mini-mart, so I ordered a strawberry shake instead.

The man who rang me up turned out to be the manager. On a whim, I asked if he knew anything about the sinkhole and the tunnel. To my surprise, he did. He was so interested in talking about it that, after whispering something to one of the kids running the checkout, he fixed my shake and sat down with me at a table.

"That sinkhole really brought in some business for a week or so," he began. "There were cops and FBI and canine drug-sniffers and even two guys from the university. The law enforcement people were interested in the drugs; the university guys were trying to figure out the history of the thing and the city was interested in getting it filled in and paved over. No one was talking or listening to each other until they started wandering in here and eating lunch together."

"Then what happened?" I asked.

"Nothing much. The cops and Feds stopped sniffing and the university guys flitted in and out for a few more days but everyone was afraid the whole thing would collapse any second so now it's all fenced off waiting for someone to decide what to do with it."

"What do you want them to do?" I asked again.

"I think it's a lame excuse for a historical site, sitting under a main street in a suburban business district. They should just finish sifting the dirt, take a few more pictures and then blow it up or fill it in so nobody gets hurt and the traffic can go back to normal.'

"Makes sense to me," I said. "But I'm curious. Did they find anything else in there besides the drugs?"

"Not really. They found a lantern and part of an old pickaxe. That and the wood and nails holding the thing up dated it back to the French and Indian War in the late 1750s. The only other things in the tunnel were the drugs, a bunch of cigarette butts and what the university guys described as a strong smell of urine, especially near the entrance. I suppose if someone took the time to carefully sift through everything they might find a button or a coin or a musket ball, but no one wants to take a chance on another cave-in."

"It sounds like it was an exciting time for you."

"Yeah, I guess. Usually it's pretty boring around here. By the way, how's the shake?"

I had just started slurping up the bottom of the cup so I said, "It was good enough to finish, and for a place like yours that's a compliment."

He stood up to leave but I called him back.

"One more question. I met a guy this morning over by the tunnel. He was a good-looking man, fortyish with dark hair, jeans and an olive colored polo shirt. You ever seen him? Do you know who I'm talking about?"

The manager sat back down.

"Sure, I know him. He comes in here all the time. His name's Doc. At least that's what his friends call him."

"Friends?" I asked with at least one of my eyebrows rising. "Tell me about the friends."

"Well, the one with the long red beard is hard to miss. A nice guy, though, but quiet . . . and then there's Bombo . . . that's what Doc calls him . . . Bombo. I don't know what a "bombo" is supposed to look like but I don't think he looks like one. Anyway, Bombo has only come in two or three times. He never takes off those dark glasses and he always orders hot tea. Hot tea's not even on our menu but he just says, 'Fill a cup with the sweetened ice tea and nuke it hot.'

"Doc does almost all the talking but it seems to me Bombo is the guy in charge, if you know what I mean. By the way, why are you so interested in all of this?"

"My cousin was staying down the block at her brother's place when the street fell in," I explained. "She got all interested in the whole thing so I thought I'd snoop around a little on my way to Manhattan. Thanks for the chat. I guess I got lucky and wandered into the right burger joint.

"Thanks yourself," the manager said as he got up for the second time. "It was good talking to someone who's actually interested for a change instead of the news people who just want to cover the story and go back home or back to the studio or wherever they go back to."

"I'll take that as a compliment so now we're even. By the way, if you don't mind, I might hang around and wait for some friends to show up."

The man shrugged and walked back to make sure the burgers were being flipped properly.

I phoned my friend at the NYPD . . . again.

"This is Mike, I've got another license plate for you to run."

"Mike," he said. "You can't keep calling me every few hours. I could get in trouble if my supervisor found out I was feeding PD info to a civilian."

A thought crossed my mind.

"Doesn't someone monitor your conversations?" I asked. "Is our conversation being taped?"

"Mike, I'm at home on my day off. Cut me some slack. No one's recording anything. So sit tight while I check on the plate."

I had counted to thirty-two when he came back on the line.

"It's registered to a Morgan Finster."

The name came with an address in Saratoga Springs.

"One last question," I said. "The name Morgan could be either male or female. Which is it?"

"He's 44 years old and says he's a male and I suppose he would know. That's all I can tell you."

"Thanks," I said. "I'll try not to phone you again for a while."

"That would be a nice change. By the way, you owe me fourteen cups of coffee."

"You know I don't bribe cops," I said. "You're doing this out of the goodness of your heart in a cooperative effort to fight crime."

"Sure," he said. "I'll have a latte."

The latte sounded like a good idea so when the conversation was over I ordered a coffee with double cream.

As I sipped the java, I was glad to notice that fast food restaurants were catching up with the 21st century. My phone was getting low on juice and there was an outlet right next to the table. They also had wi-fi so I plugged in my cell and began searching for Morgan Finster on the internet.

There wasn't one. Not in Saratoga Springs, not in New York, not in the United States, not in the Western Hemisphere or anywhere else . . . at least not on the internet. Either the guy had no identity apart from the DMV or he was a phony.

I *Google Earth*-ed the address and came up with what looked like marshland, without a house in sight.

The word Bombo, however, turned out to mean a lot of things including towns in Uganda and Australia. It's also a type of drum used in Argentina, a media company in the Philippines and an old musical starring Al Jolson. None of it helped me ID the guy with the name, so I found myself one strike short of three again.

Mona checked in with a text message. Since she was still two hours away and I had nothing better to do, I called up the Speedy Rental Car Company. I recognized the voice of Mr. Redhead immediately.

"Is this Speedy Rental Car?"

"Yes."

"Is this Marty?" I asked.

"Who's Marty?" came the response.

"Who am I speaking with? I'm looking for Marty."

"I'm Sam, Sam Borden if you want to know the details. What can I do for you?"

"Nothing, I guess, I was trying to find Marty. He ran away from the Home for Mentally Disturbed Children and someone said they thought they saw him around your place. If you see him don't get too close but call the police, okay? Thanks."

I hung up.

Finally, I had a name with real potential.

It turned out Sam Borden was a well-known sports writer for the New York Times. Unfortunately, that particular Sam Borden was beardless, did not live in Albany and was not employed by a rental car company.

I didn't want to push my luck with my old contact at the NYPD so I called up a gal I know on staff with the NY Department of Corrections. She's helped me with criminal info before so I thought I'd see if she had any leads on Sam Borden. It turned out she did.

"He's got a long record of misdemeanors and one felony conviction for having 3 ounces of cocaine under the front seat of his car. A judge threw out the conviction because the cop had pulled him over for running a red light and didn't have enough reason to search the car. Borden has spent time in city and county jails but never in a State Penitentiary."

His address matched the location of Speedy Rentals.

"Thanks," I said. "I needed that."

"Mike," she added, "you owe me at least four steak dinners. When am I going to collect?"

"You know I don't offer bribes," I said. "You're doing this out of the goodness of your heart in a cooperative effort . . . ."

" . . . and blah, blah, blah," she interjected. "You've handed me that line before and it sucks like a Dust Buster. I'll take mine medium rare."

That gave me an idea. Maybe I could call everyone I owed food or coffee or vacation trips to the Bahamas and pay them all off at the same time with an evening at one of those "all you can eat" buffet places. I thought about it, but I knew I'd never get around to doing it.

None of it mattered anyway. At the moment, my only concern was Robert. I didn't think anyone was going to hurt him and I didn't think he was being held for ransom, either. My guess was when the bad guys finished cleaning up and putting away whatever they were doing, they'd let him go and then disappear. On the other hand, I knew I could be wrong, and that was worrying me a lot.

Time to go to the cops, I told myself, so I did.

Fifteen minutes later I was standing at the enormous front desk of the central Police Station asking to talk to whoever it was who headed up the narcotics division. After a very short wait, I was ushered to the much smaller desk of Officer Marco Inoye.

"I've got some info on the narcotics stash you found in the tunnel last July."

"Go on," he said as he pulled a pen out of his shirt pocket.

I explained everything that had happened except for the bit about the journal and the possibility the tunnel extended further down the street.

For Inoye the important details were: 1. The three men who seemed to be involved, 2. The Speedy Rental Car Company, and 3. Robert and Sonja—One, two, three in that order.

My priorities were in a different order of course but I gave him my business card and promised not to screw up his investigation. After we shook hands,

I headed back to the front desk to file a missing person report on Robert.

As soon as I was finished, my phone beeped twice. There was a text message from Mona asking where to meet; and one from Connie saying she and Joe had stopped at a gas station in East Greenbush to use the restroom. Both cars were about ten minutes away.

I gave them directions to Budget Burger and hurried to get there before they did.

The manager was nice enough unlock the Party Room so the five of us could have a quiet place to talk.

Sid's car and Joe's Miata pulled into the parking lot like Stanley and Dr. Livingstone converging on each other in Central Africa.

I felt nervous for the first time since being kidnapped in Florence. I felt nervous because I had ordered everybody up to Albany and couldn't think of any reason for them to be there.

It was 4:45 p.m. when we gathered in the Party Room. After a quick round of introductions, everyone listened as I filled in every detail I could think of.

I waited for someone to ask the infamous question and after a few awkward moments of silence, Chia provided it.

"What do we do now?"

Mona, who is sharper than the key of E Major, came up with the first idea.

"You said someone installed a manhole entrance to the tunnel in the vacant lot, right?"

"Yes," I said. "Why?"

"Because if the . . . what did you call them . . . the bad guys know about the other half of the cave they might have put another entrance in the other empty lot. We may not be able to see it but if it's got metal in it we could find it with a metal detector."

Yeah," said Joe. "I bought one of those things once. I looked for treasure all over the place but all I found was some loose change on the high school football field. Those things are bogus, for sure."

"Thank you, Joe," I said as nicely as I could fake it, "but I think Mona has a good idea. I wanted to check out the lot but was afraid to go by myself. I didn't want to disappear like Robert and Sonja. If all five of us went over to look for the tunnel entrance there wouldn't be much anyone could do about it except shoot us and that wouldn't be a good idea because it would just get them into even more trouble. So I say, let's do it. For all we know, Robert could be down in that tunnel somewhere."

"Don't forget the gold, Mike," Connie said, apparently missing the whole reason I had called everyone up to Albany. "The gold might be in there, too."

"Sure," I said. "You can look for it after we find Robert."

"Where do you rent a metal detector?" Mona asked.

"At the metal detector store, maybe?" Joe suggested.

"I saw a rock shop next to the Interstate," Chia said, ignoring Joe's comment. "If they don't have one I bet they'll know someone who does."

I started to say, "Let's do it," again but didn't, because apparently it finally hit home to Chia that Robert was really missing and she started bawling. Connie looked down at the floor, embarrassed. Joe looked around as if he was thinking about buying something to eat, and Mona, of course, took Chia in her arms and held her. I have no idea what the two of them talked about during the long drive to Albany but I suspected Chia had left more than a few tearstains on Sid's upholstery before they pulled into the Bargain Burger parking lot.

Since everyone else was either worrying about Chia or trying to ignore her I *Yelped* "rock shops" in Albany and quickly found the one Chia had mentioned, mostly because it was the only one in town.

I tapped the phone number and the man who answered said they closed at 5:00 p.m. on Wednesdays but he could rent me one in the morning when they opened at 9:00 a.m.

"No thanks," I said. "I need it now and I'll give you $100 if you'll stay open long enough for me to pick it up in five minutes."

"It's a deal," the voice said. "but you can keep your $100. I'll be here sorting things out for another half-hour anyway, so just stop by before 5:30 and I'll work something out."

"Joe," I said. "This is something you and Connie can do. It would be a big help. Besides, Joe has had experience with metal detectors before."

Connie knew I was blowing volcanic ash but figured it was better for her and Joe to do something useful instead of sitting around at Bargain Burgers smelling the onion rings burning in hot oil and waiting for Chia to stop crying.

When they were gone, I joined Mona in putting an arm around Chia.

"It's going to be okay," I said. "Nothing is going to happen to Robert."

"You don't know that," she said, starting to sob in earnest again. "For all you know he's dead or in Canada going over Niagara Falls in a barrel. You don't know anything so just shut up. If anything happens to Robert I'll never forgive you . . . never!"

Mona looked at me with eyes wide and moist. I could tell she was feeling sorry for me and didn't want to pile more guilt onto my head than I had already put there myself.

I asked the manager to nuke some sweetened ice tea for Chia. After a few sips she started to calm down.

"Mike," she said. "I don't blame you for any of this. Robert's a grown man and free to get into whatever trouble wants, whether you set him up for it or not. If I blame anybody, it's got to be Robert. The two of you really do make a good pair and I know you want to find him as much as I do."

Mona smiled at me and I did my best to smile back. In my heart, though, I knew I would never really smile again until we had brought Robert and Chia back together.

As far as I could tell there were only two leads we could follow . . . at least when it came to finding Robert.

The first lead was to follow Sam "Redbeard" Borden around and see if he went anywhere or did anything that gave us a clue to something.

The second lead was to locate the entrance to the other half of the tunnel . . . if there was one . . . and see where it led.

Normally I would be the person to follow up on both leads but now that I had a posse, I needed to allocate my resources in the most efficient way possible. Time was being lost by the minute and I couldn't afford to lose a single whiff of its essence.

"Mona," I said. "Except for me, you are better than anyone else in the room at following people around without being noticed. I've seen you in action and you are good; really good at it. So . . . I want you and Chia to drive over to Speedy Auto Rentals and follow Sam or Doc or Bombo or anyone else who looks useful to see where they go. Whatever you do, do not get out of your car. We don't need another victim . . . ." I looked at Chia and decided I should have chosen a less upsetting word. " . . . I mean we don't need another disappearing act. So keep your distance."

" . . . and be discreet, right?" Mona finished.

"Right."

"When do we start?"

"Now would be good. It's already 5:20 p.m. but there's a slight chance Sam's still there, or maybe someone else is there. We won't know unless you go.

"I want Chia to go with you because the two of you make a good team. I also happen to think that Sam is our best chance of finding Robert and it would be nice if Chia was on the team that found him."

I drew a map with directions and after we switched keys, they headed towards Chia's car.

"Wait a second," Mona said as she stopped and turned around to look at me. "You and Connie are going to go into that vacant lot by yourselves? Do you think it's safe? After all, it will getting dark soon."

"You're forgetting about Joe," I said, "the guy with muscles for brains. Unless he's a coward he'll be perfect. Besides, I don't think he's smart enough to be a coward anyway."

Mona winked and was gone.

I was alone again, spinning ideas the way a spider weaves webs, hoping one of them would catch something tasty enough to turn into a meal.

A few minutes later Joe and Connie walked in.

"We've got the detector in the car," Connie said.

"Yeah," said Joe. "It didn't fit in the trunk and the Miata doesn't have a back seat so Connie had to hold it in her lap with the handle sticking out the window. It was kinda cool how she figured out how to do it."

"Yeah, Joe. Really cool," I said as insincerely as I could.

Connie shot an unpleasant look in my direction but I deflected it with a smile.

"Let's go hunting," I said.

"Go hunting for what?" Joe asked in clueless sincerity.

"Hunting for Robert, you dumb ass!" Connie said as she socked Joe in the arm hard enough to make him wince.

Chapter Thirteen

Like Sacks of Wheat
Wednesday Evening

We could have walked the 300 feet to the vacant lot but we took Sid's car instead. We needed the car in case we had to make a quick getaway. A second reason was that walking along the street with a metal detector would have attracted a lot of attention. The one thing we didn't need was to attract a lot of attention.

When we stepped into the blackberry bushes Joe reached for the detector. I told him that since he was so big and strong I needed him to stand nearby and look for trouble. Connie shot me another dirty look but took the detector back from Joe and handed it to me.

"I'll stand with Joe," she said.

I paced off the distance shown on the map and stood within ten feet of where the opening of the original tunnel should have been. Within those ten feet, there was nothing to see but two maple trees and a complete lack of ground cover. If there had ever been an entrance there, it wasn't there now.

I flipped the switch on the metal detector and followed the invisible squiggly line in the journal all the way back to where the tunnel had caved in. Apart from some old tin cans and assorted scrap metal, the detector didn't register a thing. Visually, there was nothing suggesting that anybody had been rearranging the ground to either build or cover up a high traffic manhole entrance.

When I came back to where I started Connie walked over to have a chat.

"Mike," she said, "there's someone standing in that small clearing on the far side of the lot. You can't see him now but he's somewhere near that big tree. I'm not sure but I think he's watching us. He's making me nervous. Maybe we should leave. Besides, it's getting dark and creepy."

"I don't like the dark, either," I said. "But give me ten or fifteen minutes and then we'll back off. Tell Joe he's doing his job really well and I couldn't be doing this without him."

"Sure," Connie said, "and I'll tell him you're nominating him for *Time Magazine*'s 'Man of the Year' while I'm at it."

"Go ahead," I said. "You know if you say it he'll believe it."

"Shut up, Mike," she said as she turned and walked away.

I turned the detector back on and this time, instead of following the line of the tunnel I walked away from it, making a wide sweep of fifteen feet on each side. For twenty feet I found nothing. Then, where the lot started sloping down into a ravine, there was a "beep;" and then another, and then a soft squealing sound that wouldn't stop until I turned the thing off.

In front of me, the ground was bare and trampled. Scattered around was the sort of debris someone might push off the back of their truck instead of taking the extra time to haul it to the dump. I could see an old refrigerator, a shredded mattress, an old door and some plywood sheets that looked especially suspicious.

I waved Joe and Connie over and said, "It's here somewhere. I know it. But it's getting too dark and there are only three of us. There's that guy over by the tree and there could be others we can't see. Who knows, there could be a half-dozen more in the tunnel waiting to pull us under if we were dumb enough to open their front door. I don't want to quit when we're this close but I don't think we have any choice."

We walked back to the car and decided we would take turns sitting in the Miata watching the area in case someone went in or out. After volunteering for the first shift, Joe walked back to the burger place and brought his car over. Connie offered to sit with him but I was afraid temptation would distract them from keeping their eyes where they needed to be, so Joe did his shift solo.

I planned to relieve him in two hours and then Connie could take a turn. The two who were not on duty would sit nearby in Sid's car and try to sleep.

I shot a text to Mona and Chia telling them what we were doing. It had been nearly an hour and a half since they drove off and I hadn't heard a word from them. I texted them again telling them to text me back. When they didn't I began to worry.

I tried not to let Connie know how close to panic I was. Fortunately, she was in the back seat where she couldn't see my teeth gnashing.

I didn't want to phone Mona because if she hadn't put her phone on vibrate the ring tone could give her away to someone nearby. Despite that concern, I was so anxious I started to phone her anyway.

Before I could hit the "Call" button, a text message beeped in. It was Mona.

"*Mike,*" it said. "*Sam leaving in truck when we got to Speedy. Followed him to bar in Scheenkepdy. He went inside. now short, stocky man with dark glasses came out together. Both got in truck and driving your direction. Will follow. 143.*"

I was glad to see Mona had activated her auto-spell app.

Maybe there was going to be a showdown after all.

For the second time that week, I wished I had brought the handgun I keep in my office desk. When I take it with me somewhere, I never need it, and when I need it . . . nuts.

I forwarded Mona's text to Joe with a personal note telling him to stay in the car no matter what happened. I was assuming he could read.

For nearly ten minutes, we sat waiting for something to happen.

Then it happened.

A blue pickup sailed past us like a blur and stopped on the far side of the sinkhole next to the other vacant lot. Someone came running out of the dark and jumped into the back of the truck just as it sailed off in another blur.

Right behind them came Chia's car, going so fast it was obvious they were following the pickup. My guts were screaming that this was not going to turn out well for anyone.

Chia and Mona followed the truck as it turned onto a cross street heading south. For a moment we could hear the roar of engines revved to the max and then . . . nothing. The sound stopped. Not like sound fades away when it disappears into the distance but like sound stopping dead in its tracks as though cut off by a pair of scissors.

Frantically, I started Sid's car, floored the accelerator, skidded through a u-turn and squealed around the corner. Chia's car was in the middle of the street, directly in front of Connie's brother's house. The car lights were on, the engine was softly purring, the two front doors were open and the front end was slightly crushed . . . as though it had run into something or something had backed into it.

More to the point, the girls were gone.

What have I done? What have I done?

If I was holding a crowbar I would have beaten myself on the head with it.

Connie, who had been asleep in the back seat, was screaming and swearing, "What the . . . what the . . ." over and over.

"Shut up, Connie. We're too late. They got away."

"Who? . . . What? . . . Too late for . . . Who got away?"

When I explained what happened she screamed even louder . . . until the tears choked her into silence.

I told Connie to get up in the front seat and park Sid's car next to Joe's Miata.

"I'll be there in a minute," I said as I walked over to Chia's car.

Inside I found Mona's phone, lying on the floor in front of the passenger seat. The phone was still lit up, displaying an unfinished text message.

"We think Robert Sonja back of truck murphy too fstss . . . ." it said.

How the hell did Robert and Sonja get into the back of the truck? And who the hell is Murphy? I screamed to myself.

"Mona!" I screamed, but this time I screamed aloud so the whole world and God could hear it.

"Mona!"

I sat in the driver's seat of Chia's car and wept.

When the crying was over I drove back to be with Connie and Joe.

"It's time to call the police," Connie said. "Right away. Right now."

"Call 911," I said. "Tell them where we are and tell them it's life or death."

While Connie talked to the dispatcher, I grabbed Joe, handed him the metal detector, scrounged two flashlights out of the cars and headed through the blackberry bushes to the backside of the vacant lot.

By the time Connie caught up with us, I had already flipped over a square of plywood, exposing a metal manhole cover neatly fitted into a small precast concrete vault.

"Pull it out, Joe," I ordered.

When Joe lifted the cover, we saw a metal ladder disappearing into the darkness below.

"Idiots first," I said quietly as I stepped into the hole.

There was nothing at the bottom but dirt and darkness. It was as quiet as a jet engine is loud. I could hear my heart pounding and could smell the hint of urine as I waited for Joe and Connie to join me.

We stood at the beginning of a tunnel. Here the walls and ceiling were shored up by wood beams and old railroad ties. On the ground was trash and debris of all kinds as if someone had been living there.

Connie stopped suddenly and grabbed the back of my shirt.

"Mike," she whispered as if she was in a cathedral, "what's that?"

It was Robert's wallet and cell phone sitting on a small piece of torn newspaper. There wasn't any money in the wallet but his driver's license and credit cards seemed to be untouched.

Had Robert been in the tunnel? Or just his stuff?

I didn't know the answer one way or the other, but now we knew without any doubt that whoever had been in the tunnel had been connected with Robert's disappearance.

I stuffed the wallet and phone in my pockets and kept walking.

Twenty feet further the tunnel widened and we found ourselves surrounded by an odd, musty smell that hinted of mildew, rot and decay.

Here the wood was old and bent, held together with square nails. Further on, where the tunnel came to an end was a pile of small cardboard boxes sitting on top of a wooden plat.

I handed my flashlight to Joe and carefully opened one of the boxes.

Inside was a thick, clear plastic bag that gleamed like the Crystal Cathedral in the dim light.

"Meth," I said without any emotion in my voice whatsoever. "Crystal meth . . . damn."

To her eternal credit, Connie didn't say anything about gold.

We exited the tunnel at the same time the first police car arrived.

It was exactly 8:00 p.m.

Connie and Joe stood to one side as I gave my report to the responding officers.

Upon hearing what we found in the tunnel they immediately called Officer Inouye along with everyone else assigned to the narcotics division. Then they called the FBI.

They wrote down everything I had to say about Robert, Mona, Chia, Sonja, Speedy Rental, the blue truck, Sonja's motorcycle, the car chase, the tunnel, everything, in fact, except the journal, which I still kept as a now-unimportant secret. By the time we finished with the interviews the first of the narcs were arriving with the local FBI agent trailing close behind.

"What the hell were you doing, going down that hole on your own," Inouye scolded when he finally arrived. "It could have been booby-trapped. There could have been thugs down there. You could have died. What is wrong with you, Maurison?" and so on.

I deserved all of it . . . every word, but I didn't care. I had told everything I knew to law enforcement and there was nothing left for me to do except answer the same questions over and over again until everyone was satisfied they knew all the answers.

After thirty minutes, my knees gave out and I collapsed onto the ground with a groan. Joe and Connie sat next to me and this time it was Joe's turn to ask the now-famous question.

"What do we do now?"

It was the first intelligent sentence I had heard him speak all day, but none of us had an answer.

The first person into the tunnel was a member of the bomb squad looking for things that go "boom."

When he didn't find any and signaled the "all clear," Inouye and his crew slithered down to take a look. They were there a long time before one of them came up for air. He asked for every DEA agent on the East Coast to join the clambake as quickly as possible and the G-man did the same for the FBI.

Soon the area was lit up like Times Square on New Year's Eve and almost as crowded. The three of us were completely lost in the shuffle so we walked down the street to Bargain Burgers to talk things over.

The first thing Joe did was order a triple bacon cheeseburger and "hold the tomatoes."

Connie and I just sat down at a table, exhausted and emotionally numb.

On a whim, I dialed Chia. It came as no surprise when she didn't answer so I left a short message on her voice mail:

"Chia, we don't know where you are but we're not saying anything to the police yet. Tell Mona we'll be trying to figure everything out on our own. Take care. Bye."

My hope was that Doc, Sam and Bombo would listen in, hear the cops weren't on the case and be tricked into thinking they were home free. Since everyone I knew and loved was backed into one corner or another, Mike's Survival Rule #3 had been worth one final try. This time, however, I hadn't lied for Mike's survival but for Mona and my friends.

My guts groaned at the thought it had been the final try so I quickly amended my feelings to allow for as many additional final tries as possible.

When I put my phone back in my pocket, my hand bumped into something that shouldn't have been there. What I pulled out was Robert's wallet. In my other pocket was his phone.

When I turned it on it beeped as all the emails and text messages that had been sent since it had been turned off were downloaded.

The battery was down to 10% but there was enough juice left for me to prowl through the texts and emails before it went dead. The emails weren't relevant and the text messages were all familiar except for one from Mona and an unfinished text from Robert that had never been sent.

Mona's text had been sent and received the previous morning: "*Hey, how's it going with you and Mike? If you bring him back by this afternoon I'll kill a fatted calf for both of you.*"

The unfinished text said, "*They have sonja and I . . .*" and that was the end of it.

At 9:00 p.m., the officer assigned to the missing person division *Bolero*-ed me with a phone call. In two minutes, he and two other officers walked into the burger place and joined us at our table.

"Can I get you a soda or a coffee?" I asked, "or maybe a shot of whiskey?"

"No thanks," the officer said. "I've got a thermos half-full of it in my patrol car."

He didn't explain what was in the thermos but since I was too tired to make a wisecrack about it he got lucky.

Because all three purported abductions had taken place in or around Chia's car, the officer seized it as evidence. I gave him the keys and we both signed a receipt for the transaction.

Joe spent the entire time mindlessly eating his burger. For the first time all day, Connie looked like she was wishing she had left him back in Worcester.

I had photos of Robert and Mona on my phone and Mona's phone had several of Chia, so the police had some good descriptions to use at the start of their investigation.

When the officer saw that Mona's phone and mine had exchanged texts with Robert as well as with each other, he confiscated them, too. Reluctantly I handed over Robert's phone and wallet as a bonus.

"How am I supposed to keep in touch with anyone?" I asked. "My phone has all my contact phone numbers and email addresses on it . . . not to mention my calendar and appointments . . . ."

"Sorry about that, Pal. If you follow us down to Central, I might let you copy down the ones you need the most. But don't worry, we'll keep it charged up and take any calls that might come in. If it's for you we'll take down the message and pass it on."

"Thanks," I said. "You're a dear."

The officer was empathizing like a pro, so he let the snide comment pass without comment.

After jotting down Connie's number as a point of contact he excused himself and left the restaurant with the two officers who had come in with him.

When Joe finished his burger, we followed everyone outside. Joe and Connie climbed into the Miata and I cranked up Sid's car. We followed each other to the Central Police Station and sat around for the next two-and-a-half hours in case we were needed for something.

No one offered to get us a cup of coffee and no one offered to get me a shot of whiskey, either. I was so thirsty I wouldn't have cared what was in the officer's half-full thermos. I would have downed it all in one breath.

By Midnight, the only two people left were the desk officer and the dispatcher. The last investigator to leave put his arm on my shoulder and said, "We'll be in touch."

I was not comforted.

Using Connie's phone I called Mona's parents and then Chia's parents to let them know the situation. These were two of the most difficult phone calls I ever made, but each family needed to know the score in case they were contacted by their daughter, a law enforcement officer, the media or one of the bad guys. Besides, I didn't want them to hear about it on the evening news. I called Robert's parents last. They didn't answer so, although it wasn't a very pleasant way for them to hear the news, I left a message on their answering machine.

Connie then called Aunt Lucille and, when that call was over, she called her brother Ben.

Ben told her he had heard two cars racing down his street earlier that evening. He had looked out the window in time to see two women being hustled out of their car and tossed into the back of a pickup truck by two men.

"Like sacks of wheat," is how he put it.

He had phoned 911 five minutes before Connie did, which explained why the cops started showing up so fast. Ben said an officer had interviewed him but he had no idea who was involved in the incident or why all the sirens and flashing lights appeared at the end of the street. When Connie explained it to him over the phone, he was speechless.

When Connie mentioned we were bouncing around an empty police station like dots in the old Pong video game, he invited the three of us to spend the night at his place.

When we got there Joe made a move to go into the guest room with Connie, but Connie pushed him out and closed the door in his face. Since I claimed the sofa first, Joe got a blanket and an air mattress on the floor.

None of us slept well except for Joe, who snored louder than Robert.

As I lay on the sofa, I thought about the last long conversation I had with Mona before our lives had started to unravel. The conversation had been about faith.

"I guess I'm stuck with you," Mona had said. "The Bible says you're supposed to be my "help-meet" in faith as well as life. So here's your chance."

It dawned on me that right now might be my last chance to be a "help-meet" for Mona. Her life was out of my hands but maybe I could do something about the faith part of it.

Mona said she had faith in me . . . because she believed there was faith in me already.

"You have more faith inside you than you think," she said.

I couldn't argue the point. After all. if there was even one crumb of faith in me, it was going to be more than I thought I had. Now, however, I needed to dredge up as much of it as I could find.

"Think about it," she had said. "Pray about it. Pray about it any way you like. Use words if you have to. Just talk to God . . . ."

I could only remember three or four times when I had ever prayed to God before now. Each time I had felt hopeless and powerless in the face of some crisis or other.

As I considered my options, I realized how inadequate my Survival Rules had become.

#1."When in danger: Run."

At the moment there was no place for me to run.

#2. "When in doubt: Stay where you are."

As above, there was no place else to go even if I wanted to.

#3. "If you're caught in a corner: Tell a lie—the bigger the better."

The only lie I could think of was the lie that I was in control of anything at the moment.

When in danger, when in doubt . . . .

There was little I could do except wallow in self-accusation and pity. The only other option was to pray.

I took a deep breath and thought about how I should go about doing it.

When I was on my honeymoon, I decided God knew my thoughts before I ever put them into words. Now, as I lay on the sofa, I believed God had already heard the prayer of my heart.

Yet Mona had said, "Use words if you have to," so with my back to the wall, I used words.

"God," I said. "I know I really screwed up everything and now I'm scared and alone and worried to death. Dear God, help Mona get out of this jam, and Robert and Chia, too . . . and Sonja. Wherever they are keep them safe and set them free. Can you do this? Can you do it for me? Please? For all of us? That's what I want and I can't do it by myself. Maybe the police can do it but it would be a big help if you stepped up to the plate, got a hit and brought them home."

I paused, realizing that turning God into a major league baseball player was maybe just a little over the top, but I had said pretty much all I had to say, anyway. After the pause, I simply added the word, "Amen," as if it was a period, or maybe an exclamation mark at the end of a sentence.

I didn't think God was going to be hung up on the grammar angle so that didn't worry me much. More important, somewhere deep down inside of me, I knew my prayer had been heard.

What I didn't know was whether it was going to be answered.

Chapter Fourteen

Forgive Me
Wednesday Night

Eventually I fell asleep, but each time I dozed off it would only be a few minutes before I woke up again. Each time I woke up, I found myself hoping for morning; but morning never seemed to come. I would stare at the ceiling and listen to Joe's snoring until I drifted into the land of dreams again.

There were no worms in my dreams that night.

Instead, every dream featured Mona in the starring role with Robert and Chia as the supporting cast. For some reason my character had been written out of every scene. So I paced nervously back and forth in the wings, waiting for an entrance that never came.

As I waited, I rehearsed my lines until the words were etched into my memory as deeply as the wounds of unrequited love are etched into a lover's heart.

"Mona," I would say as I fell on one knee, "I'm sorry for being such a fool. Forgive me and give me another chance at being your husband. I know I don't deserve you, but I love you. Say yes to me Mona. Please say yes!"

In my dream, I waited for my scene to arrive, but my cue never came. The play went on without me. The audience laughed and the audience cried. When the curtain came down there was a standing ovation, and when the players took their bows, the people threw flowers onto the stage.

I watched it all from behind the scenery where no one could see me. I was invisible, as if I had never existed. I cried out to get Mona's attention but instead of words, only silence flowed from my lips— a silence lost amid the sound of applause.

In my dream, I walked through the backstage door and into the alley behind the theater. It was dark and I was alone. In the Green Room, the Cast Party began with champagne and laughter.

No one missed me, and every time I woke up, I felt as though I had lost Mona and my friends forever.

Chapter Fifteen

Marmalade
Thursday Morning

When the light of the sun finally reflected on the living room windows, I awoke feeling sore, exhausted and hungry. Except for the milk shake, I hadn't had anything to eat since lunch the day before.

My head and heart would have preferred to pull a blanket on top of my head and stay on the couch pretending to be asleep, but my guts, growling with hunger, didn't agree.

When the ballots were counted, my guts won handily, because the rest of me stayed on the sofa and didn't even make the effort to fill out an absentee ballot

Ben and Mindy were already in the kitchen tending to the incoming alimentary demands of Sam and Susan.

I had slept in the clothes I had worn the previous two days and probably looked like a refugee from Goodwill Industries, but Ben greeted me with a quiet, "Good morning," and handed me a cup of coffee.

"Thanks," I said.

I felt like Dylan Thomas must have felt when his pen screamed out the words,

> *Do not go gentle into that good night.*
> *Rage, rage against the dying of the light.*

Inside I was raging but on the outside, I was too tired to show it.

Connie came into the kitchen next, bright, clean and fresh having just taken a shower.

"Mike," she said. "I had nightmares all night and kept waking up when snakes started coming up through the manhole when Joe lifted the cover off. I hope you slept better than I did."

"Thanks for the encouraging words," I said, "but I had nightmares of my own and I don't really want to think about them at the moment."

Turning to Ben I said, "I'd really like a piece of toast or an English muffin with some marmalade if you have any."

"Coming right up," Ben said. "I've got both so I'll make you one of each. The marmalade is peach, by the way. I hope you don't mind."

"I won't mind anything," I said, not exactly sure what I meant by it.

"Hi, y'all, and g'mornin'!"

The voice was loud and under the circumstances, inappropriately cheerful.

"Good morning, Joe," Connie said without a trace of enthusiasm.

Joe looked at me and paused for a moment, as if he had suddenly remembered what had happened the day before and why he was there.

"Hey, Mike," he said at last, in a tone of voice that was surprisingly appropriate for the occasion.

I gave him a short nod of recognition, added a second spoonful of sugar to my coffee and sat down at the table across from Sam and Susan.

From then on, all the chattering came from the two toddlers. Listening to them made me feel as if life might still be worth living. I've never understood why parents are so hesitant to bring small children to funerals. Death and life are best celebrated together and nothing represents life better than toddlers like Sam and Susan.

When I had prayed the night before, I hadn't asked God for smiles or laughter but, like the toast and English muffin, I wound up getting both. Maybe

God is good after all . . . in spite of the mess we humans seem to make of everything we touch.

Mona, of course, believes "God is good all the time" and "All the time God is good." When it comes to little children, she may be right. When it comes to grown-up drug dealers, she may be wrong. But then again, just because one person is bad doesn't mean that no one else can be good. No matter how bad things might get, there will always be the possibility of goodness just around the corner, like light shining in the darkness.

At that moment, my world was so dark I needed all the light I could get.

Thank you, God, I said silently from the depths of my soul. *Thank you for Sam and Susan.*

I hadn't realized I needed a blessing, but when I got one, I was grateful for it.

Ben brought the toast and English muffin and set them on the table alongside the marmalade.

"I can't believe it's happened," he said. "It's so weird to think I was watching Mona being taken away last night and I didn't even know it was her."

I don't need to hear this right now, I thought as I took a bite of muffin.

"I only met her once, and that was at Dad's funeral. At the wedding I don't think I even had a chance to say "Hi" but from what I could see she must have been really special."

God may not be a stickler for grammar but when Cousin Benny relegated Mona to the past tense, I steamed up so fast I knocked over the jar of marmalade. It rolled slowly out of reach towards Sam and Susan. When it came to the edge of the table it paused for a melodramatic moment before plunging to the glazed tile floor and shattering into a million pieces.

I was too embarrassed to vent my anger at Ben but the thought of Mona being in the past tense made me feel sick to my stomach.

While Mindy and Connie started cleaning up the mess, I headed straight to the nearest bathroom. As soon as I closed the door, I bent over the toilet and threw up.

When I came out everyone pretended the bathroom door had been soundproof except Joe.

"I bet you feel a lot better now, don't you Mike?" he said as he handed me his half-eaten donut. "Here, have a bite. It tastes real good and I don't mind sharing, seeing as you're not feeling very good for, you know, reasons and everything."

If I had been packing heat, I would have burned him on the spot, so it turned out that leaving my .380 in the desk drawer was a good thing after all. The awkward pause, however, gave me a moment to reconsider what had just happened

No one was ever going to confuse Joe with Miss Manners but at least he had been thoughtful enough to offer me his breakfast. Maybe his edges were a little rough and maybe his social graces were on life support but since his heart seemed to be in the right place, I cut him some slack.

After counting to ten and remembering I was a guest in my cousin's home, I took the donut, said "Thank you," walked outside for some fresh air and tossed the donut into a bush.

I was feeling better already.

"I'm sorry about the mess," I said, after I calmed down and came back inside. "I guess I'm just . . . ."

It's all right, Mike," Mindy assured me with a wink. "The children do things like that all the time."

Mindy smiled at me in a way that said, *We're going to keep loving you whether you like it or not.*

The choice was easy . . . I decided to like it.

A hint of a smile forced its way onto my face. I gave Mindy a wink of my own and immediately felt awkward and embarrassed for having done it. Mindy's smile turned into a grin as she winked back. Then, as she began humming a song to herself, she turned and started wiping the food off her children's faces.

How odd that life could still be normal for someone else when my own life had spun completely out of control. The resentful part of me cried out, *It's not fair,* but the rest of me found comfort in knowing I had looked around the corner and found that goodness was still there after all.

Joe, seeing how nice Ben and Mindy were being to everyone, took advantage of the situation and asked for a Denver omelet and hash brown potatoes. Ben stared as his watch for a long time before he started cracking eggs into a bowl.

With everyone else occupied, I called Connie over and asked her to step out on the front porch with me.

"What is it?" she asked once we were outside.

"Nothing," I lied, realizing I had a bad habit of avoiding straight and honest answers to simple questions. "I just wanted to ask you about Mona's text message; the one she didn't send."

"What message was that?" Connie asked. "You never mentioned it."

"I found it on her phone and I didn't want to forget it so I wrote it down while we were sitting at the police station."

I pulled a scrap of paper out of my pocket and handed it to Connie. On it, I had copied down the last message Mona had sent and the one she had left unsent on her phone.

Mike, Sam leaving in truck when we got to Speedy. Followed him to bar in Scheenkepdy. He went inside. now short, stocky man with dark glasses came out together. Both got in truck and driving your direction. Will follow. 143.

and

We think Robert Sonja back of truck murphy too fstss . .

"What does '143' mean?" she asked.

"It's a short way of writing 'I love you.' The numbers match the number of letters in each word."

"Oh," Connie said. "I've never seen that before. It's very sweet."

"Tell me about the first text. What do you see?"

Connie read and reread the words carefully before she offered a translation.

"It's not particularly cryptic," she began. "When Mona and Chia drove up to Speedy Car Rental they saw Sam getting into the blue truck and followed him as he drove away. It seems to me they assumed Sam was the only person in the truck."

Connie paused as if to consider something before starting up again.

"Then they followed him to Schenectady where Sam parked the truck and went into a bar. It doesn't sound like they pulled into a parking lot so Sam probably parked the truck on the street. I suppose the girls did the same with Chia's car."

"Yeah," I said. "That's how I read it too, but here's the interesting part. The bed of the truck didn't have a cover on it so if there had been something . . . or somebody lying in it anyone

152

walking past on the sidewalk could have looked in and seen it. That means that when they arrived in Schenectady, the back of the truck was empty. Does that make sense?"

"Yes," Connie replied. "I was assuming that already."

"And then . . . ?"

"Well," she continued, "sometime later Sam came out of the bar with a guy with dark glasses. I don't know for sure but it sounds like the same guy the burger manager called Bombo. Next, the two men got into the truck and started driving back towards Albany and . . . you know . . . where we were sitting and watching the vacant lot."

At that point, I took over the narration.

"A few minutes after Mona sent the text, the blue truck zipped past us. It stopped just long enough for someone to jump in the back . . someone who had been standing in the shadows of the other vacant lot. We don't know who it was but we can guess it was the same person you saw watching from behind the tree when we were searching for the tunnel entrance. We can guess it was probably the guy called 'Doc,' right?"

"So far so good," came Connie's response.

"That means," I continued, "there wasn't time for anything or anyone to have been put into the back of the truck before they drove past us and headed down this street with Mona and Chia following close behind . . . ."

" . . .and," Connie cut in, "like Mona said in the next message, Chia was going fast . . . at least I assume that's what 'fstsss' is supposed to mean. What do you think?"

"Yes," I said. "It wouldn't make sense any other way . . . but here's the thing I can't figure out. Mona says,

We think Robert Sonja back of truck.

"How could she say that, when there was no way for them to be in there? The only person in the back of the truck was 'Doc' and Mona probably wrote the text before the truck stopped for him to jump in. It doesn't make sense. I don't get it. What do think?"

"I think it has something to do with 'murphy,'" she said. "Maybe murphy was in the truck somewhere or maybe murphy is a bed or maybe murphy was 'too fast.' I don't know for sure, but it must have something to do with murphy."

"That's what I think, too, but it's a real puzzle and I don't think the police are going to spend much time on it. They seemed a little overwhelmed by everything last night, so if anyone is going to figure this out in the next few days it's going to be us."

"So . . . ," she started to say.

" . . . what do we do now?" I finished the sentence for her.

"That's not what I was going to say," Connie said with a snip in her voice. "I was going to say, why don't we look up the word 'murphy' on the internet alongside the words 'Albany'and 'Schenectady?'"

"It can't hurt," I said, "but I don't have a phone anymore. Will yours work? or should we ask Mindy or Ben to use their desktop?"

"Mine will work," she said as she pulled out her phone, "and Joe's will work, too, if we need it."

After a short pause she said, "Damn, my phone's as dead as a doornail. I'll go and get Joe's."

In a few seconds, she was back on the porch typing into Joe's phone.

"Hmmm," she hmmmed after the results popped up. "There are a number of 'Murphys' listed in both places. Most of them are last names. It would take a while to sort through all of them."

"Try the word, 'Murphy's' with an apostrophe in front of the 's'," I suggested on a whim.

"Hmmm," Connie hmmmed again. "This is interesting, There's a Murphy's Tavern in Schenectady. Maybe that's the bar Sam went into, but what does that have to do with the back of the truck? Mona doesn't even mention any of it in chronological order. What was it about the car chase that made her think of Robert and Sonja and

Murphy and the back of the truck all at the same time?"

"That's another good question but I think the only place we'll find an answer is in Schenectady."

Before we left to pay a visit to Murphy's I used Joe's phone to call the Museum of Modern Art and let them know Robert was going to be tied up for a few days. Then I phoned the Hunter College Library and told them Mona was laid up for the rest of the week, and last, I phoned the beauty salon in Greenwich Village where Chia works and told them she wasn't coming in to work, either.

"Here," I said as I tossed the car keys to Connie. "You drive. That way you can drop me off at the curb while you find a place to park."

"What's the hurry, Mike? It's not even 9:45 a.m. and according to the phone, Murphy's doesn't open until eleven."

It was yet another question I didn't have a good answer for.

"I suppose we could stop by the Speedy Car Rental on our way into town."

"Why do you want to go to a car rental place?" Joe asked as he came through the door and onto the porch. "We've already got two cars."

A few minutes earlier, I had felt like taking Joe out with my .380 and now, judging from the expression on her face, it looked as if Connie wanted to finish the job by strangling him.

"I don't want to rent a car," I explained, using as many one-syllable words as I could. "I just want to take a look around in case Robert left something behind when they grabbed him. Or maybe we'll find something else that will help us figure out where everybody is."

Joe shrugged and said, "If that's what you're going to do then I might as well go with you. I don't have anything else to do anyway except drive back to Hartford."

Joe had just offered a self-description that seemed to fit him so perfectly he could have carved it onto his gravestone as an epitaph:

I don't have anything else to do anyway . . . .

Perfect.

When we took a moment to say "Thank you" to Ben and Mindy, Ben slipped something into my shirt pocket with a wink of his own. It turned out to be a cigar. After the three of us piled into Sid's car I took it out of my pocket and stuck it in the glove compartment for later. After that, it was only a seven or eight minute drive to Speedy's. As I expected, there was no one there.

"Closed Until Farther Notice," said a sign in the office window. The misspelling made me smile for the second time that morning. It felt good to smile but there was a slight twinge of guilt attached to it. It made me wonder if Mona, Robert, Chia or Sonja had smiled since they'd been taken away. If so, what might have caused them to smile? The only way to find an answer to that question was for me to find them and ask them myself.

We walked back to where I had found Robert's car parked in the shade.

"Here's where Robert was when he got out of the car and looked around. According to his last texts, he saw the vacant-lot guy, who must have been 'Doc,' and then a minute or so later, he saw Sonja.

"What we need to do is for each of us to pretend we're Robert and then go where we think he went and do what we think he did and then stand where we think he might have been when he said he saw things. Try to create the best scenario you can. If you find something that could be a clue, it will be a bonus, okay? Good luck."

I heard Joe whisper to Connie, "What does 'scenario' mean?"

In a louder whisper, I heard Connie say, "It means keep your eyes open."

"Oh," Joe replied. "I thought it meant like to make up a story that sort of makes sense out of what happened to Robert, but whatever . . .but why would Mike need to say 'keep your eyes open?' If I didn't keep my eyes open I couldn't see anything and I'd walk into things."

"That's the point," Connie said.

Connie and I started walking in more or less the same direction while Joe wandered off onto the property next door; property that was completely cut off from the Speedy lot by a cyclone fence.

To each his own, I thought to myself. *At least he's out of the way.*

As we walked towards the building, Connie veered off to the left towards the back of the rental office while I kept going straight, passing in front of the office where I could have seen inside the garage if the door had been open.

My guts started telling me I had gone the wrong way.

"Robert would never have put himself out in the open like this," they said. "It would have looked too suspicious."

My guts may be annoying at times but they are rarely wrong. Maybe Connie had the better idea. It made far more sense for him to sneak around the back before coming around to sneak in the front.

I was turning to walk over to Connie when Joe yelled out a "whoop" that was probably heard a block away.

"What's going on, Joe?" I asked as I turned back and stood facing him with the fence between us.

"This is a big shoe," he said, pointing at the ground. "Connie said Robert is a big man." He moved his head back and forth as if he was trying to shake the rest of the sentence out of it. "It's a new shoe so that means it hasn't been there for very long."

Joe was right. The shoe was one that Robert was wearing. But why was it on the wrong side of the fence? Why had it come off? Why did he leave it behind?

Connie, who had hurried around the rental building when she heard Joe's "whoop," joined us by the fence.

"Maybe Robert walked over there so he could get a clear view of the office and the garage without being seen?" she suggested after she had looked things over.

"Maybe he was knocked out from behind and his shoe came off?" I added.

Next, it was Joe's turn to speak.

"If he's a big man and got knocked out they'd have to drag him somewhere and there isn't anything that looks like someone was dragged anywhere."

Joe was starting to make more sense than I would have thought possible. It was all confusing but the shoe was there, which meant Robert had probably been there, too. It also meant that when he saw Doc and then Sonja he was probably standing at that same spot sending me a text. What happened next we'd have to find out from Robert, if we ever found him . . . or from Doc or Sam if they ever turned up.

I told Joe to step back so he wouldn't mess up the footprints more than he already had. Then the three of us walked along the Speedy side of the fence. We didn't see anything else that looked suspicious.

"Leave the shoe where it is," I said. "Connie, call the police and tell them what we found. Tell them where to find the shoe and tell them we didn't touch anything."

After she made the call, she snapped a few photos of the shoe and the area around it, "just for the record."

As soon as she put the phone back in her jeans pocket, it rang.

"Mike," she said, "it's for you."

It was an Albany police officer, the one assigned to monitor our phones.

"Is this Mr. Maurison?" he asked.

"Yes," I said. "I'm the guy. Why?"

"Everyone's been trying to reach you all morning but no one answers. We've left messages but you haven't called back. Whose phone are you using now?"

"Joe's," I said. "You must have gotten his number from the call Connie just made. By the way, what do you mean 'everyone's been trying to reach me all morning?'"

"I'm not sure, that's not my job. All I have is a message for you from someone named William. He didn't sound very happy but this is what he said:

"'Maurison—you SOB—Leslie McGillicutty is a *man*, dammit, a stud male. I don't know who the hell you followed but it wasn't Leslie McGillicutty, and where the hell are you, anyway? I can't afford to lose any more toilets so step it up. Time is money for both of us, so if you want to see any money you're going to have to spend more time doing your job.'

"That's it; that's the message," the officer said. "Sorry about the language but I guess that was part of what he wanted you to hear. I hope it makes sense to you because it makes absolutely no sense to me."

"Thanks," I said. "Nice talking to you."

So . . . it was Leslie Neilson after all.

I glanced at my watch.

"Time to head over to Murphy's," I said. "If we get there when it opens I might have a chance to talk to someone before the joint gets busy."

It turned out I didn't need to worry about the place being busy.

Murphy's was tucked away in what appeared to have once been a thriving industrial area. The bar fronted a street with an abandoned railroad track running down the middle and the building behind it was a large brick warehouse with nearly every window broken. On the back side of the warehouse was the Mohawk River.

There were four or five pickups and cars parked along the street. A neon sign advertising beer was lit

162

up in the tavern's window next to a smaller one that beamed out the word, "Open."

"The sign says it's open so I guess I'll go in. Park the car over there across the street. If I don't come out in thirty minutes, I want Joe to come in and look around. Joe, if you don't see me anywhere don't do anything or say anything to anyone. Just walk straight back to the car and tell Connie to phone the police. Do you understand what I just said?"

"I understand," he said, "but thirty minutes in a bar isn't even enough time to sip one beer. You're going to be guzzling for sure."

"That's my business, Joe," I retorted. "Your business is to do what I told you, right?"

Joe nodded.

"See you both in a few minutes," I said as I stepped out of the car and headed towards Murphy's front door.

On the way, I noticed one of the cars had a bumper sticker that said, "Murphy's Tavern," on it.

Good advertizing, I thought as I went through the door.

It was so dark inside I wouldn't have known if it was day or night if I hadn't just walked in from the late morning sunshine.

The walls were covered with dark-wood paneling, interspersed with brick pillars. The tables were covered with vintage yellow Formica and on the ceiling were orange glass lampshades that looked as if they'd been hanging there since the late 1960s. In the back corner where it was darkest, there was a pool table. One of the side bumpers sagged enough so that a hard hit ball would have flown up in the air and hit someone in the eye if they weren't paying attention to the game.

Smoking in bars has been illegal for a long time, but Murphy's still reeked of it, probably because the walls, ceiling, floor and carpets hadn't had a good cleaning since the mid-90s.

It didn't seem to be the sort of place that served specialty micro-brewed beer. It didn't seem to be the sort of bar that had a lunch or dinner menu, either. Whatever food they served probably came out of a can or a bag of some sort. Pretzels and peanuts were probably the featured appetizers during Happy Hour—if they had a Happy Hour.

The only customers were two men sitting at the bar. I joined them and told the bartender to bring me a cold mug of the house draft.

"Nice place," I said.

"Nice what?" the man two stools away asked.

"Nice place . . . the bar . . . in here," I said a little louder.

"Oh, it sure is," he said. "I've been coming here for over 40 years, back when this whole part of town was humming like a bee in a bottle. Those were good times and the beer was better back then, too, wasn't it, Doc?"

"I wouldn't know," the man on the stool next to him said. "I wasn't alive then."

As he turned his head to speak I could see he was the same man Robert and I talked with two days earlier when we were standing next to Sonja's motorcycle. I quickly turned my head away so he wouldn't see my face. If Doc recognized me, Joe would probably end up looking for me in the bar after all. Personally, I wanted to walk out of Murphy's long before Joe walked into it.

Maybe I should leave now, I thought, *or maybe I should stay and check things out for a few more minutes.*

Since I hadn't finished my beer and since I hate to waste a good brew I decided to stay.

It turned out to be a mistake.

For some reason the image of a bumper sticker popped into my head and a light bulb lit up like in a cartoon when someone gets a brilliant idea.

Oh . . . my . . . god . . . I whispered to myself as I suddenly realized Mona's last text made perfect sense after all.

"We think Robert Sonja back of truck Murphy."

It wasn't Robert and Sonja who were in the back of the truck, it was a bumper sticker—a bumper sticker that said, "Murphy's Tavern." Mona must have seen a "Murphy's" bumper sticker on the back of the blue truck. She realized the tavern was not just a place where Sam had gone to get a beer and meet Bombo, it was where Robert and Sonja were being held as prisoners. That had to be what Mona was trying to say. It was a good clue, but we'd missed it . . . and now it was too late.

As if on cue, the bartender slowly made his way around the bar and placed himself between the front door and me. He was at least six-foot four and must have weighed a muscular 250 pounds. The good thing was, he was smiling. The bad thing turned out to be the short stocky guy with dark glasses that snuck up and tapped me on the back.

"Hi, Mike," he said. "How nice of you to stop by. Consider yourself a guest. The beer is on the house."

Doc and the other man stood up and I found myself pinned against the bar counter like a sheep about to be sheared.

"Uh, thanks for the beer," I said.

I had started to say, *Thanks for the beer, Bombo*, but under the circumstances I figured the less I said, the better chance I had of getting out of the bar alive.

"I understand you have some friends who have gone missing," Bombo continued. "It's all over the papers this morning and everybody's talking about it. Let's see, there's Mona, and Chia, and Robert and . . . no . . . don't tell me, I'll remember . . . and . . . and *Sonja* . . . that's it, *Sonja*.

"I suppose that's what happens to people when they stick their noses into other people's business. If they aren't careful, they could get their noses broken, or an arm, maybe. You wouldn't want that to happen, would you, Mike?"

"No," I said, "I hate it when things get broken. As a matter of fact . . ." (*I stood up and checked to see if there was enough space for me to get past the bartender and make it to the door . . .*) " . . . at breakfast this morning . . . " (. . . *before being body slammed to the ground.*) " . . . I knocked a jar of marmalade onto the floor . . ." *(I started counting, One, Two . . .*) " . . . and it shattered into a million pieces." (. . . ***THREE!***)

On "Three" I threw what was left of my beer in the bartender's face and ran towards the door as if my life depended on it . . . which it probably did.

I hadn't gone two steps before a gun went off and one of the orange light fixtures exploded into pixie dust.

I stopped running as quickly as I had started.

"Good choice," Bombo said.

I was still facing the door and, although I couldn't see anyone, I could sense the bartender building up steam like a pressure cooker. No one likes to have cold beer thrown in their face . . . and bartenders are no exception.

"Bombo," I said as I turned around slowly with my hands in the air, "Let's talk this over, and this time the beer's on me."

167

I took a step forward . . . right into the bartender's fist. I wasn't conscious long enough to leave him a tip.

When Joe walked across the street to check on me twenty minutes later he found the front door locked. As he stood wondering what to do next, the two neon lights flickered off and a third one flickered on.

"Closed," it said.

Like my eyes.

Chapter Sixteen

I'm Not Sam
Thursday Afternoon

I was either in another darkened room or my eyes were still closed; I couldn't tell and I didn't really care. Everything was quiet, like a library where all you hear is the soft hum of the air conditioning system breathing life into the stacks.

The thought of a library made me think of Mona and I began thinking about what she was doing at work today and what time we'd have dinner later this evening.

Something was bothering me but I couldn't put my finger on what it was. Everything was so quiet—too quiet, in fact. Where in New York City could I be where it was so quiet? The museum? No, that didn't make sense, why would I be lying on my back in a museum?

I felt something on my nose and reached my hand up to touch it. My nose felt tender, wet and crusty all at the same time.

"Mike?"

The name was spoken in a whisper.

"Mike? Are you awake?"

"Sure," I said in a whisper of my own. "Why are we whispering? Is it a secret or . . . ."

I felt my arm go limp. My hand fell across my chest and I drifted off into my own personal silence again with the word, "Mike" echoing in my subconscious.

Who was Mike? Was it me? Or was my name Nesbit? Did it matter?

"Mike, wake up, it's Mona."

I felt the touch of a hand on my forehead.

Mona. The name sounded familiar . . . *Mona . . . works at the library . . . Mona and Mike . . . Mike and Mona . . . Mike Maurison, Private Eye . . . .*

I sat up like a catapult flinging a boulder at a castle wall.

"Mona? Is it you? They let you go? Are you all right? . . . Oh, Mona!"

I rambled the words but my eyes were still closed.

"It's me, Mike. I'm fine and so are you. Robert and Chia are here, and Sonja, too. We're all here together."

I could hear several voices say, "Hey, Mike" and "Greetings and salutations."

That last line must have been Robert, but his voice sounded so far away.

"Welcome to Murphy's Country Club and Spa."

The voice was definitely Robert's, but what was Murphy's Country Club and Tavern? . . . But Robert didn't say 'tavern,' he said, 'spa.' Where did I come up with the word 'tavern?"

Tavern!

I opened my eyes, and there was Mona up close and personal, smiling a smile awkwardly attached to a face that was otherwise etched with concern and pain.

Consciousness returned with the subtlety of a nuclear explosion. All the details of the past week careened through my brain like a data-burst passing through a top-secret NSA communications system.

I remembered everything and re-experienced every conceivable emotion simultaneously.

It all passed in a moment but when it was over, I felt more awake and alert than I had in a long time.

The brick-walled room was lit by one low watt light bulb dangling from the ceiling. The space looked like a large storage room with empty metal shelving on the walls and a pile of broken cardboard boxes stacked high in a corner.

Most important of all, Mona was there along with our two best friends.

Mona's left arm was in a sling, Robert's face was bruised and there was the dark silhouette of someone lying curled up next to the cardboard.

"*Buenos Tardes*, Mike."

The voice came from behind me. It was Chia and for the first time I realized someone's hands were on my shoulders, apparently making sure I didn't pass out again and keel over backwards.

"*Buenos nachos*," I said with a smile that made the center of my face burn with pain.

"I think you broke your nose," Mona explained.

"That," I said, "is what happens when you stick it in someone else's business."

"By the way," I added, "We found Robert's shoe. Sorry I didn't bring it with me."

I felt strong and steady enough to stand up, and with Mona's and Chia's help, I did.

"What do we do now?" I asked—a question that brought on an unsettling feeling of *déjà vu*.

"We wait for the cavalry to arrive, Colonel Custer," Mona said, imitating my penchant for sarcasm. "We were hoping you'd bring some troops but it looks like you left them back at the Little Big Horn."

"I brought them," I said, "but I left them sitting in Sid's car parked across the street from Murphy's. Connie and Joe are in the car and they saw me go in but by now, they know I didn't come out. With any luck they've already called the police who will arrive any minute, seated on steaming stallions with sabers raised."

"They must not be riding very fast," Mona replied. "You've been lying here unconscious for almost three hours."

I looked at my watch. It was 3:15.

"It's still Thursday afternoon, right?" I asked.

It was.

"Where are we?" I asked.

"In a basement," Robert said.

"I can see that," I said. "But where's the basement?

"We have no idea," said Chia. "When they threw us in the truck Mona broke her arm . . . at least we think it's broken . . . and Doc flopped himself on top of us until we pulled to a stop.

"'Close your eyes,' he said, "so that's what we did."

"You closed yours," Mona interjected, "but I took a peek and saw what looked like a darkened street with old, rundown, brick buildings everywhere. There was an alley of some sort and at the back end of it I could see lights shining a long way away. The lights reflected on water so I assumed we were somewhere alongside the Mohawk or the Hudson.

"Then Doc, or Sam or the other one, grabbed my arm. The pain was so intense I almost passed out. From then on my eyes were closed."

"You did good, Mona," I said. "It sounds just like the street Murphy's is on or close to it. If I was Bombo, I'd want to hold us within spitting distance."

"My guess," I continued, "is that Sam is outside the door making sure we're not going anywhere. I think it's Sam because Bombo and Doc were sitting in the bar when I came in. The bartender and another, older guy, were there too and seemed to be partners in the whole thing."

"So," said Chia. "What's been going on? What have we missed?"

"Well for one thing, you're all famous."

I went on to tell how Ben watched as Mona and Chia were pulled from the car and how we discovered the tunnel filled with crystal meth. I mentioned how the police confiscated our phones and Chia's car, and described how Connie and I finally deciphered the text messages. Finally, I told them I had made phone calls to everyone's parents and work places . . . except for Sonja.

"Sonja!" I said suddenly. "Where's Sonja?"

"Over there," Mona said, pointing to the curled up figure by the cardboard. "Apparently she didn't play along with Simon Says so she's been tied up like a rodeo calf ever since we've been here. The cords aren't cutting off circulation or anything but they're knotted so tight the only way to get them off would be with a knife. She's not gagged, but we have to spoon feed her. She doesn't say much except when she has to go to the bathroom, and we have to help her with that, too. It's almost like she's catatonic or in deep shock. Either that or she's just mad at everybody, including us."

I went over and whispered a few words into Sonja's ear, trying to explain what was going on and letting her know we could really use her help. She was breathing but other than that, there was no sign she even heard me.

Then it was Chia's turn to talk. She told how everyone's wallet was taken away, and how Mona and Chia were each given their purse back because they were filled with all their girl things. Sonja's backpack was lying next to her as well, still bulging as though it was still full.

There was water and toilet paper and an old-fashioned chamber pot for everyone to poop and pee in. I assumed someone emptied the pot every so often or the room would have smelled like a pit toilet.

"That's about all of it," Mona said, looking around the room, "except for the cardboard, the shelves, a few blankets and the light bulb."

The walls, of course, were brick. There was a small slot near the ceiling that might have been an air vent, but there wasn't any light coming through it. The only way in or out was a door next to the pile of cardboard. It appeared to be solid and heavy, made of thick slabs of oak tied together with cross-bracing. Next to the door handle was an old-fashioned keyhole—the kind that needs a skeleton key to unlock it.

"Who brings you food? And who empties the chamber pot?"

Robert stood up for the first time and gave the answer

"Either Sam or the Old Guy; probably the one you saw in the bar."

As usual, Robert didn't use more words than necessary. Since there was more that needed to be said, Mona filled in the blanks.

"When it's meal time whoever's on guard knocks on the door and says, 'Come and get it.' He unlocks the door and steps back ten feet or so holding a pistol of some kind. One of us slowly opens the door, slides the tray of food back into the room, and then puts the poop pot out for someone to empty. After we close the door, he locks it. When he brings the pot back we do the whole thing again in reverse, including putting the food tray and empty dishes back outside the door. It's the same thing for breakfast, lunch and dinner . . . except Chia and I haven't been here long enough to have dinner yet. Robert says it will probably be peanut butter sandwiches again."

"Mike," Chia interrupted, "can you get us out of here?"

It seemed hopeless. It was Little Big Horn all over again, and we were Custer surrounded by some very ticked off Native American warriors.

Were we the bad guys? or the good guys in all of this? My guess was that we were more "good" than Custer, but not much smarter . . . and the 19th century Sioux warriors were more "good" than Bongo and his crew, but which team was smarter it was hard to say. On the plus side, we weren't outnumbered as badly as Custer but on the minus side, nothing of Custer's crew survived the ordeal except for one horse.

Since we didn't have a horse our situation did not look promising.

"I don't know," I finally replied to Chia. "I'll have to think about it."

At that point, everyone imitated Sonja and lapsed into despairing silence.

After what seemed a long time I turned to Robert and asked, "What time do they serve dinner?"

"I don't know," Robert said. "I don't have a watch and, like you said, they took my phone. If you want to know, why don't you ask?"

"Sure," I said. "Why not?"

By this time, everyone was looking at me except for Sonja.

I sidled up to the door and give it two small raps with my knuckles.

"Hey, Sam," I said. "What time do you serve dinner?"

"I'm not Sam," came the voice of the Old Guy I had talked to in the bar. "The waiter will bring your food at six."

I looked at my watch. It said 4:45 p.m. That gave us a little over an hour to come up with a "Get Out of Jail Free" card. The only way out was through the door and six o'clock was going to be the last time it was going to be unlocked until tomorrow.

"Let's have a talk," I said as I gathered Mona, Robert and Chia together as far from the door as possible.

We whispered ideas back and forth until we agreed on the one that seemed more likely to succeed than the others. The downside of the plan was that either Robert or I would have to face the possibility of being shot at point-blank range during the attempt.

Both of us volunteered for the job so we had Chia flip a coin.

Robert called heads.

It was tails, which meant I won . . . or lost . . . I suppose it depended on how you looked at it.

Then we went through dress rehearsals until we had everything timed as perfectly as we could.

Chapter Seventeen

Hue & Cry

Thursday Evening

At six o'clock, there was a knock on the door.

"Come and get it," came the voice.

Chia pulled the door open wide enough for Mona to slide in the food tray and for Robert to put out the honey pot.

As Chia stepped back to close the door Mona slid a thick, stiff piece of cardboard over the holes where the latch and the dead bolt went into the doorjamb. The door held the cardboard in place when it closed

When we heard the key go into the door, we paused for a moment before we sprung into action.

The plan was based on the assumption the Old Guy would stick the pistol in his pocket or put it down somewhere when he pulled out the key to lock the door. To help things along, Robert had carefully put the honey pot directly in front of the lock so the Old Guy would have to lean across to put the key in the hole.

We figured that after he turned the key the first time and found the bolt wouldn't slide into place, he would then put one hand on the door casing to get more leverage and try to turn the key harder the second time.

It was at that exact moment I whispered, "One, two, three, *now*!"

On the word "now", Chia pulled the door open as quickly as she could. The door opened inward, pulling the Old Guy forward with his hand still holding on to the key like a vise.

I immediately charged through the opening, with Robert forcing himself through the door behind me. Together we collided with the Old Guy as he fell forward, and our momentum forced him clear across the hallway where we crushed him against the wall.

He was so surprised that, except for a faint expletive as he sagged to the floor he didn't make a sound.

Robert pulled a strip of torn blanket from his pocket and tied a gag while I knelt with my knees on the jailor's chest.

Earlier, we had switched off the light and, with Robert holding me up high enough to reach it, I pulled the light and wiring down to the floor. We had broken the wiring into two pieces that we now used to tie the man's hands and feet. We could have used our belts to do this, of course, but neither Robert nor I wanted to take a chance on our pants falling down during the get-away.

The whole thing worked like a charm—even better than we had hoped.

When we found the gun lying on the floor, I slipped it into my pocket "just in case."

The only thing left to do was get Sonja.

Earlier, when I explained the plan to her it had seemed to invigorate her to the point of talking.

"If you can't untie the ropes just leave me behind," she said. "If you get out of the building you'll be bringing help in a few minutes anyway.

"But . . . ." she added, "Whatever else you do, take my backpack. I think it still has the journal pages in it. The gold is in the tunnel somewhere and if I can't get it, it might as well be yours."

"Don't worry about it, Sonja," I said. "We'll get you out; we won't leave you behind."

"And the backpack?" she asked.

"Yes," I assured her, "we'll bring the backpack, too."

Although we searched the Old Guy's pockets, we didn't find anything we could use to cut off Sonja's bonds. A couple of well-placed bullets from the pistol might have done the job but the noise would have brought everyone within earshot running in our direction and that was the last thing we wanted to happen.

Since we had run out of ideas, Robert picked Sonja off the floor and carried her out of the room like a football while Chia grabbed the backpack. We left everything else behind.

To our relief there didn't seem to be anyone else in the building. In just a few seconds, we were out on the street trying to decide which way to go.

"That way," Mona pointed for some reason known only to her.

Since it didn't seem to matter which way we went, we followed Mona and her finger down the street as fast as we could go.

At the first intersection, we turned left, away from the river towards what looked like a well-lit cross street. It was the longest two blocks I have ever run, and it must have seemed even longer for Robert.

Every so often, we would see a car drive through the intersection so the first thing I did when we got there was to run into the street and try to flag one down.

The first three cars veered away and sped down the street as fast as they could go.

The driver of the fourth car, however, turned out to be an off-duty cop who, while driving home, was keeping his eyes open for anything that looked like a blue pickup.

Instead of the truck, he found *us*.

Within moments, he was calling for back-up. After taking one look at Sonja, he pulled out a knife and cut her loose. For the first time in three days, she was able to stand on her feet and move around. The first thing she did was to walk over to Chia and take her backpack into her arms.

"Thank you," she said as she looked around at everyone. "Thank you . . . all of you."

"Officer," I asked, "where is Murphy's Tavern from here?"

"Murphy's? It's four or five blocks that way." He pointed east down the street, "and two blocks towards the river. "We were there looking for you six hours ago, but all we found was a wallet."

So Connie had called the police after all.

I looked at my watch. It was 6:15 p.m. on a Thursday evening.

We had all nearly died . . . and for what? For gold? For greed? For stubborn pride? Yes, I figured, for all of the above.

But most of all, we almost died because we loved each other and were willing to do anything to save one another from whatever sins of commission or omission we had blundered into.

In a matter of minutes, we found ourselves surrounded by sirens and flashing lights. I thought the whole thing was unnecessary, especially since it would probably signal Doc and Bombo it was time to get out of Dodge and hole up somewhere like maybe in Canada or New Guinea, but then again, the raid on Murphy's had probably already sent them packing.

I figured they owed somebody big time for the drugs they lost in the tunnel and it was unlikely any of them would to be able to pick up a cool five or six million dollars from a local pawn shop on short notice.

The way I saw it, they were dead meat no matter what they did. Ironically, they were probably going to be better off in the loving arms of the police than anywhere else.

That, of course, was their problem, not mine. All I wanted to do was go back home and be with Mona.

Mona! I had completely forgotten about Mona!

I found her sitting sideways on the back seat of the officer's car with her legs sticking out into the street. Sonja was sitting on the seat next to her with her head resting, appropriately enough, on the back of the headrest on the seat in front of her.

Robert and Chia were standing behind the car holding both hands and resting their foreheads against each other. Since Robert is at least seven inches taller than Chia, he was bent over like a paper clip. It looked uncomfortable but I doubted either of them were thinking about it much.

I went over to Mona and got down on one knee.

"Mona," I said, "I'm sorry for being such a fool. Forgive me and give me another chance at being your husband. I know I don't deserve you, but I love you . . . ."

Before I could finish my lines, Mona reached out her right hand and laid it on my head, the way the Pope does when he gives a blessing.

"Be quiet," she said. "I love you, too, and now none of this matters, It's all over . . . ."

" . . . except," I interrupted back, " except for the hue and cry of law enforcement and the media."

As the police began to ask questions, the first thing we told them was where we had been locked up and where we had left the Old Guy trussed like a Thanksgiving turkey. This reminded me to hand over the pistol I had stuck in my pocket. After that, I gave a description of everyone I had seen at the Tavern, including Doc and Bombo, who we had already described to the Albany police.

When the first round of questions were over, they hustled us into three squad cars and provided limousine service to the Schenectady Police Station.

Until that moment, the case had been the responsibility of the Albany Police, so it took a while before it was decided where we should go. Because we'd been kidnapped in Albany, the Albany police should have had first jurisdiction, but since we had been locked up and rescued in Schenectady the crime of involuntary incarceration had taken place on someone else's turf. After a few emotional exchanges, the powers-that-be decided the folks who picked us up had first dibs, at least for the moment, so Schenectady it was.

We didn't know it at the time, but Mona's parents, Chia's parents, Robert's parents, Aunt Lucille and Sonja's mother had all driven up that morning, each of them in various states of panic, anger and concern.

It turned out Ben and Mindy's phone had been disconnected during the night when a line repair went wrong somewhere and since Connie's phone had decided to be a doornail, no one could get through to us until after the police started using Joe's number.

In any case, after thirty minutes of questioning, everyone arrived at the station at the same moment: Three double and two single sets of parents, half the Albany police force, and at least three or four representatives from every media outlet in central New York State.

The front entrance to the police station looked like St. Peter's Square in Rome during the election of a Pope. It would have taken a modern-day Moses to part the mob enough to get through without crowd surfing.

Somehow, with the help of the police, our families made it into the station by way of the garage entrance in the back. When they saw us, we rushed together, greeting one another with tears and hugs and at least one, "Mike, what the hell is wrong with you."

I had heard the question before, but this time I answered by saying, "At the moment? . . . Nothing's wrong with me. I'm just glad to be alive and standing here with Mona, my friends and my family."

The person who asked the question was Mona's father.

He seemed satisfied with my answer and gave me a big hug before adding, "You have no idea how worried we've been . . . and thank you for phoning us when you did."

When the police became aware that Mona's arm needed medical attention they hauled her over to the nearest hospital Emergency Room. Robert declined medical attention so I was the only one who went along with her for the ride. X-rays revealed a simple fracture so, while they were fixing her up with a temporary cast the attending physician took a quick look at my nose.

"Yep," he said, "It's broken. If you leave it alone it will heal by itself—but I wish I could be with you when you look in the mirror tomorrow morning."

He paused, whistled and said, "Boy, oh, boy, that's going to be one heck of a shiner!"

"If you'd like," he continued, "I can give you a full cranial cast to hold everything in place."

"What?" I asked, totally baffled by the comment.

"Your entire head will be encased in plaster but, if you want, I can put some air holes in it to help you breathe. Some patients prefer not to breathe, but whatever you . . . ."

He obviously saw the look of fear on my face and decided he had played me for a fool long enough.

"Just kidding," he said. "Forget about the cast. Just leave the nose alone and you'll be fine. I'll tape it up, but if you have any problems here's the name of a Rhinologist friend of mine who practices in Manhattan."

I considered the possibility of suing him for malpractice over the joke. After giving it some thought I decided to give him a break because, 1. It was late in the evening, 2. He was pushing a twenty-four hour shift, and 3. He probably needed to take a nap more than I did. With that in mind, I dropped the idea of a lawsuit like an aerial bomb in a war zone.

As for what my nose had to do with a rhinoceros, I had no idea.

Everyone at the police station knew it wasn't practical for any of us to go back to Ben and Mindy's place for the night because the media would have lit the whole place up with spotlights from their "On the Scene" trucks and television cameras. Instead, Connie and I sent an email giving them a personal account of our afternoon adventure. Ben replied saying if it wasn't for the kids they would have headed straight over to see us but, in any case, they were glad we were free and safe.

"Thanks for the muffin," I replied, "and sorry about the marmalade."

While Mona and I were in the ER, Robert's parents and Mona's parents put their heads together and booked six adjoining suites at an Albany hotel. When we returned to the police station, everyone drove across town and arrived at the hotel as inconspicuously as we could, considering four motorcycle cops accompanied us as an escort.

To our surprise, no one from the media hounded us at the hotel. I suppose the TV crews had to get their material ready for the Ten O'clock News, and the other reporters had to type up and email stories and photos to various newspapers and wire services. So as it turned out the deadlines turned out for our best—except for the one connected to Ben and Mindy's phone.

After showering and scrounging some clean clothes from parents and hotel staff, we gathered in the hotel restaurant at 10:45 p.m. for a late dinner.

"Hey, look at this," Robert said with a 'hallelujah smile,' "They don't have peanut butter sandwiches on the menu!"

While we sat and waited for the food to arrive, Sonja walked over, pulled up a chair and sat down between Mona and me.

"I want to say I'm sorry for blowing you off in front of my house the other day. I had gotten a phone call from a restaurant near Worcester warning me that a man and a woman had been following me around, asking questions about a quarry along the French River.

"When my Mom told me two people had stopped by the house saying they shared a mutual interest in quarries I freaked out. I guess my obsession with history and the lure of treasure got the best of me. I've never felt so out-of-control as I did that afternoon. I guess I took it all out on you.

"By the way, how did you know about the French River, the tunnel and the quarry? I found all of it in an obscure 18th century diary and cut the pages out, at least the ones that had the information on them. There's no way you could have known what I knew!"

"Sonja," I said, "as you probably know, this is my wife Mona. The woman who was with me at your house was my cousin Connie. She's sitting over there. She and her friend Joe were the only two not kidnapped this week, but she's the one who can explain how we happened to follow you into this mess."

"By the way," Mona added, "Mike accepts your apology, don't you, Mike?"

"Yes, of course," I said after being given a nudge in the ribs from Mona's good elbow.

Mona ordered the Swiss steak with peas and pearl onions. As usual, she ate the onions and pushed the peas off to the side. Why she does this at every restaurant with Swiss steak on the menu I will never understand. I've asked her about it several times but all she'll say is, "Because."

I suppose that is the same reason I ordered clam chowder and a side salad for my meal: "Because."

As I cut Mona's steak into bite-sized pieces, I started to feel giddy, the way I had hoped to feel when I gave her the flower four days before. Now, I felt closer to her than I had felt in a long time. More than anything else, all I wanted to do was to go home and feel giddy with her forever.

At midnight, we paid the bill and went to our rooms. The restaurant and staff had stayed open for more than an hour after closing as a favor to us. The hotel gave them overtime for their trouble and our parents left a generous tip so I guess it was a pretty good deal for them by the time we were done eating.

When Mona and I stepped into the elevator, she put her good arm around my waist and laid her head against my shoulder. When we got to our room she found that lying on the bed made her arm hurt, so she opted to sleep in a recliner chair, instead.

I steeled myself to be the best and most attentive husband possible and planned to sit next to her all night in case she needed something, but I made the mistake of trying out the pillows on the bed and didn't move again until Mona woke me in the morning.

Chapter Eighteen

Like a Raccoon

Friday Morning.

"Mike? Are you awake?"

Where had I heard those words before? Was I dreaming them or . . . .

"Mike, wake up."

They were words whispered into my ear by a familiar voice . . . it was someone I knew well, but who was it?

I opened my eyes and there she was . . . Mona, the girl of my dreams, my bride for life and my companion in crime. As always when I open my eyes in the morning and see Mona it is love at first sight.

"Hi," I said. "I'm glad we're not kidnapped anymore."

"Why?" Mona asked.

"Mona," I said, "that has to be the dumbest question ever asked. Why do you think I'm glad we're not kidnapped anymore?"

"Because you get to sleep in a bed instead of on the floor?"

"No," I said, "it's because I get to go home with you."

She bent over to give me a good morning kiss but bumped her arm, cringed with pain, staggered across the room and sank back into the recliner chair with tears in her eyes.

"Mike," she said, "I'm glad we're not kidnapped anymore, too."

As I walked over to help Mona get dressed for breakfast, she looked me in the eyes and started laughing.

"What's so funny," I asked.

"You look like a raccoon," she said

I looked in the mirror and the first thought that came to mind was that the ER doctor would have really enjoyed seeing what I was seeing.

At 8:15, we joined the rest of our entourage in the area where the hotel claimed to serve a full, complimentary breakfast. It was a good breakfast but it would have tasted even better if the price of the free food hadn't been added into to the cost of our room.

As they say, there's no such thing as a free cigar—or a free breakfast . . . unless you're staying at Ben and Mindy's house.

Today, the Albany police were going to have their turn interrogating us. Schenectady's finest had squeezed so much info out of us the previous day it would be a miracle if there was anything left to cough up for Albany.

The parents decided they weren't needed any more so when breakfast was over they checked out of the hotel, hugged us good-bye, and left.

On our way to the police station, we were again under a police escort with two motorcycles in front of Joe's Miata and two taking up the rear behind the four of us in Sid's car.

"Why all the motorcycles?" Joe asked after we parked and were walking into the now-familiar building.

"Because," said one of the police officers standing nearby, "there are bad people who would be happy to hurt you so you won't be able to testify against them in court."

"Why would we want to do that?" Joe asked.

"Do what?" the officer asked in return.

"Testify against somebody in court," Joe said.

The officer stopped and opened his mouth to say something but didn't. Instead, he looked at Connie the way people attending a funeral look at the widow and say, "I am so sorry for you."

The interrogations got off to a good start when someone brought in the coffee. There is no coffee in the world as thick and black as the coffee cops drink when they're hanging around home base. Why this is I don't know, but I'd rather drink one cup of honest police station coffee out of a Styrofoam cup than a gallon of the gourmet stuff they brew at caffeine franchises—even if they gave it to me *gratis.*

During a break in the questioning, it was announced the police had arrested the bartender who busted me in the nose. With the Old Guy already in custody that left only Doc, Sam, Bombo and the blue pickup truck still on the loose. Their photos and info were already appearing on "Most Wanted" lists all across North America. It wouldn't have surprised me to hear that "America's Most Wanted" was already putting a story together for an upcoming show.

By the time lunch rolled around, the police and the DA had done their worst and let us out of school early.

"I suppose you're free to go home, now," the chief investigative office said. "When we want you to answer more questions or need you to come back to Albany we'll let you know or, if we have to, we'll issue a subpoena.

I expected Joe to ask, "What's a subpoena?" but he didn't.

Sonja got all of her things back including her motorcycle, which the police found still sitting under the tarp in the Speedy garage.

Chia and Mona got their purses and Robert and I got our wallets back with everything intact except for some cash. The cops found my wallet under the bar at Murphy's Tavern after getting Connie's 911 call.

When I asked if we could have our phones back he said, "Since we've already downloaded everything on them, sure, why not."

Chia asked if she could have her car back.

"No, not yet. We've got to get paint samples from the front bumper so we can try and match it with the blue pickup if we ever find it."

"Oh, well," Chia sighed to Mona, "It looks as if Robert and I are going to have to hitch a ride back to the City with you guys."

"Three's a crowd," I said, "but just like in college basketball, four is fantastic."

"Oh, by the way," Robert said, "Could I have my shoe back? The one I lost at Speedy's?"

The officer thought about that for a while before deciding, "No. It's evidence you were actually where you said your kidnapping took place. We'll have to keep the shoe."

"I guess that's all right," Robert said. "I put a pair of tennis shoes in the back of Chia's car. I can wear those."

The officer held up his hand.

"I almost forgot. We took everything out of the trunk except the spare tire. If you want your tennis shoes back I'll have to get the plastic bag we put all your stuff in."

After Robert finished tying his tennis shoes, we made our way outside. As we walked out the door the large clock behind the front desk said 11:45 a.m. A moment later, all seven of us stood in the warm September sun, together for the first time by ourselves.

As if choreographed by some cosmic comedy, Chia, Mona and Joe spoke up at the same time and said, "What do we do now?"

By now, the question had become such an old joke that everyone burst out laughing except, of course, for Joe, who looked around as though he had missed the punch line.

"I've got an idea," I said. "Before we hit the road let's have lunch over at Bargain Burgers. We can tie up loose ends and see what's going on at the tunnel."

Everyone agreed and in a few minutes, we were standing under the Bargain Burger sign.

Chapter Nineteen

A Holy Place
Friday Afternoon

"Let's check out the tunnel before we eat," Sonja said. "That's what got us in trouble in the first place. Besides, I want to know if they found anything in there besides the drugs. If there's gold I'd like to know about it."

We walked past the sinkhole and stood on the sidewalk like steers at a cattle crossing, unwilling to step over the long strand of yellow crime scene ribbon that surrounded the vacant lot. It was a barrier seemingly as impregnable as the Great Wall of China.

"Hey, Mike!"

The words came from someone sitting at a card table set up near the tunnel entrance. Whoever it was, he must have had good eyesight because we were a good fifty feet away.

It turned out the man with the eagle eye was Inouye, our old friend and head of the APD Narcotics Team.

"I'm glad you all made it through alive," he said after he walked over to us. "With Mike involved I wasn't sure how it was going to play out.

"By the way," he added, looking around at everyone but me, "has Mike been inside any tunnels lately?"

"Not that I know of," said Sonja, completely unaware Inouye and I had shared this conversation before, "But he did get a peek inside this one and we'd all like to do the same if you'll let us."

"You came at a good time," he said. "The FBI and DEA have already cleared out and my men have stopped for lunch. The two profs from the university are back again, checking to see if they can figure out if this tunnel's any different from the other one. I'll let you walk over and if they say it's okay, I'll let you go down and look around for a few minutes. Since you're the ones who discovered it, I suppose you should get a chance to see what it looks like."

After a few words back and forth through the manhole, two men emerged from inside.

The first one out, balding, grey-haired, and holding a hat, put out his hand and looked around trying to decide who to shake hands with first.

"I'm, Dick Morthon," he said. "That's Morton with an 'h' after the 't'."

It sounded as though he had spoken that line a million times, perhaps since before he even learned how to talk.

"I'm the history prof from SUNY Albany, and this is my friend and colleague, Bruce Beck. Bruce likes to dig in the dirt like a three-year old."

True to form, the archaeologist's fingernails were filled with dirt, and his face was lit up like a child on Christmas morning.

"Hi," He said. "I hear you're the ones who found the tunnel. Well done! It's a treasure down there."

"Treasure?" Sonja said with eyes sparkling.

"Yes," he repeated, "a treasure and a real treat. Dick and I are going to have to bring in some grad students to help us with this one. Come on down and we'll show you what we've found so far. But don't touch anything or you'll be forced to sit through Dick's "History of Sandusky" course as punishment."

Dick smiled at the poke, as if he had heard it almost as many times as he had to explain the spelling of his name.

As we were being gestured towards the tunnel entrance Sonja announced she had something to say.

"Mr. . . uh . . . Professor Dick and . . . ."

As a PhD student, Sonja wasn't sure whether she should address them as peers or as tenured gods. Since neither professor had any idea who she was, it really didn't matter to them one way or the other. Sonja seemed to catch on to this in time to take a deep breath and start over.

"Before we go into the tunnel there's something you need to know. I should have shared it with you two months ago when I found this."

She held out a small manila envelope, which Bruce took with a curious expression on his face.

"In the envelope are several pages I cut out . . . I mean I stole from the manuscript section of the New York City Library. They're from a diary written by a man named John Bedlow who fought just north of here at the Battle of Lake George in 1755."

She reached over, pulled one of the pages out from the rest and pointed to the paragraph that told about the tunnel.

"I'm working on my PhD in History and my thesis is on that particular battle, with an emphasis on the contribution made by the New Hampshire volunteers. When I read Bedlow's reference to the tunnel, I recalled reading the story about the sinkhole and what you found in it.

"I should have called you right away but there's a drawing on the side of the page with a squiggly line and a ✠ next to it with letters that appear to say 'gold buried here.'"

As we all listened, she went on to describe how at first she thought the line was pointing to the paragraph that told about the tunnel but after reading what the professors had found she decided it was a map of a road or a river instead. She told about her unsuccessful search for a 'quary' along the French River. Then she described how she eventually concluded it had been a map of the tunnel all along.

The two professors stared at Sonja, stared at each other and then started shuffling through the journal pages again.

Connie picked up the story from that point and described how she and I unwittingly became Sonja's shadow and how we figured out there had to be more to the original tunnel than was exposed by the collapse.

Sonja added some more of her story, describing how she began searching the vacant lot for a second tunnel entrance and was confronted and abducted by Doc.

Connie then filled in the rest of our story up to the point where Joe lifted the manhole cover.

Last of all, I described what we saw when we went in the tunnel.

I could hear Officer Inouye groan when he remembered how nuts I had been to barge into the unknown darkness by myself.

"That's about it," I said, "but we're still interested in what the ✠ is there for, and what the letters 'bried gld' mean. You haven't found any gold in the tunnel yet, have you?"

"No," Dick laughed, "We haven't been looking for it, but who knows."

Bruce carried the thought further.

"If it had been the other section of the tunnel I would have laughed at the idea, too. Dick and I already guessed what the journal confirms— the tunnel was built to store military arms, not gold. No one in their right mind would have been carrying gold around with them in the wilderness back then, especially with a war going on. Besides, except for travelling a long way north or a far distance east or south there wouldn't have been anything to spend it on anyway."

"But," said Dick, obviously thinking aloud, "from what we've found this morning, it's possible that gold might have been in this new section at some point. Your map of the tunnel and the question of when it was drawn are very interesting.

"Bruce," he asked, "does this drawing look like it was drawn by the same person who wrote the journal?"

"I can't tell from looking at the 'squiggly line; that could have been drawn by anyone, but looking at the letters and numbers written in the margin I would say no, it was drawn a long time later.

204

"People, you see, learned how to write from what were called 'copy books.' The style of forming letters in the seventeen hundreds was very different from the early to mid nineteenth century. The later date is when I think the map was drawn. Maybe Dick could explain it better than me, but as far as I can tell, the letters in the margin could have been written by Abraham Lincoln, Stephen Douglas or John Brown's body for all it matters . . . ."

". . . and that," said Professor Dick, "is one of the reasons this is all so interesting to us. Come down the ladder and we'll explain."

One by one the two professors, the seven of us, and Officer Inouye went down the ladder and stood, crammed together at the narrow place where the tunnel began.

"Further down the tunnel," Bruce explained, "the beams and nails match those of the collapsed section perfectly. Like your map shows, the two sections must have been joined together when they were first built but somehow became separated later."

"That's something we'll have to take a closer look at as we refine our search," Dick added.

"Where this tunnel ends, Bruce continued, "we've already found three musket balls and a bent and rusted ramrod used in old-style muskets. This seems to corroborate the journal's description of the tunnel's use as an armory of some kind during the French and Indian War.

"But this end of the tunnel is different. For one thing, it uses railroad ties. This is important because a steam-driven railroad built with steel rails wasn't built until shortly after 1800 in England or Wales somewhere. In the United States, the first commercial railroad didn't get started until 1828 near Baltimore. The section of tunnel we're standing in couldn't have been built until much later, when railroad ties were common and old ones were already being replaced.

"So," Sonja asked, "when was this part built, and why?"

"That's what we were trying to figure out," Dick answered. "Just a few minutes ago we found an American coin with the date 1852 on it, some rusted chain and other items that could be from that period or much later. We'll have to run tests to date them accurately. It's all so interesting, and these are things we found sitting on the surface. Who knows what's underneath?"

"Gold, perhaps?" I asked.

"Maybe, maybe not," Bruce replied. "Dick and I haven't had time to talk about it yet but my guess is this entrance section of the tunnel was built in the early to mid 1850s for some reason we haven't figured out, yet. Maybe this end of the tunnel had also collapsed and someone wanted to dig it out and use it again. Or maybe the original tunnel dead-ended over there, and when the other section fell in and cut this end off someone dug a new entrance get back in."

"Bruce," said Dick, "I agree with you about the dating, but the details of how and why this new section was built, that's for an archaeologist to figure out."

"Well," Bruce concluded, "that's what we've come up with so far. This journal is extremely interesting and we're grateful you finally decided to share it with us."

Sonja looked down at the ground and said, "Remember, I told you I stole it from the New York City Library. I actually cut the pages out of the diary. I still can't believe I did that. I must have been out of my mind, but the point is, it doesn't belong to me . . . or to you, either. It's got to go back."

The silence that followed was broken by Connie.

"What you said reminded me of something: The journal may have been written by John Bedlow but there was a different name written inside the cover, as if it had belonged to someone else at one time. I didn't recognize the name and never bothered to look it up. That was really dumb of me because I suppose he could have been the person who drew the map."

"What was the name?" Dick asked.

"I can't remember exactly. I'd have to go back and look at it again to be sure, but it was Stephen something. Stephen Moore, or Moyers . . . something like that. I'm sorry, it's probably not important anyway."

"It might be very important," said Dick. "Was the last name Myers by any chance? Stephen Myers?"

"Yes, that's the name . . . Myers . . . at least I think that's what it was. I can't be positive but yes, I think that's the name I saw, but how did you know? How could you have guessed a name like that?"

"Because," Dick said, "that name ties all the loose ends together. If you're right then we've stumbled onto a very important part of American history."

"Who's Stephen Myers?" Bruce asked. "I guess he wasn't an archaeologist or I would know who you're talking about."

"No," Dick said, in a tone of voice he probably used when he gave lectures, "he wasn't an archaeologist, he was an abolitionist."

"A what?"

The voice was Joe's. It was the first time he had said anything since we parked the cars at Bargain Burgers. Part of me was impressed he was still paying attention.

"To answer your question, Stephan Myers was born a slave but was given his freedom here in

208

Albany, nine years before slavery was abolished in New York in 1827. He became a leading advocate for the abolition of slavery throughout the United States. As early as the 1830s, he was smuggling runaway slaves from the South through central New York and into Canada. Historians credit him with being one of the early leaders of what later became known as the 'Underground Railroad.' He also started an abolitionist newspaper and published it for many years. That's one reason we know so much about him, because he wrote about himself in his articles."

"Now I think I know who you're talking about," Bruce added. "I read that a local historical group discovered that one of the buildings he lived in was still standing and they want to turn it into a historical site or a museum."

"Right you are," Bruce said. "I'm on the Board of that society and that's one of the reasons I know so much about Stephen Myers."

"But what does any of this have to do with the journal or the tunnel?"

This time it was Mona who asked the question.

"I'm not sure," Dick answered, "but my hunch is that Myers came across the old diary somehow or someone took it to him and showed him the note about the tunnel. I don't know what happened next, but when that squiggly line was drawn the tunnel was still intact and maybe it was drawn by Myers himself. Maybe the tunnel collapsed soon afterwards and Myers built the new entrance, perhaps to use that end of the tunnel as a place to hide runaway slaves. There were bounty hunters from the South who searched for them everywhere. They were ruthless and sometimes grabbed any African-American they came across and dragged them back to the South whether they had ever been a slave or not.

"Myers knew all this, of course, so hiding escaped slaves on their way to Canada became an important part of the Underground Railroad, especially in the mid 1850s and early 1860s, right when this section of the tunnel was probably built. What a fascinating theory! If it's true, this will add a whole new chapter to the history books!"

"But," said Connie, "there's still the ✠ next to the map with the words, 'gld bried hre' Could Myers have stored gold in the tunnel to help finance the whole business? It must have cost a lot of money to run the slaves north and there had to be money set aside somewhere."

"I don't know, you may be right," Dick said. "What about you, Bruce. What's your guess?"

"Let me see that map again," he said.

He looked at it closely and pulled a small measuring device out of his pocket. After what seemed to be a few silent calculations, he walked to where the new section of the tunnel joined with the old and began pacing away from us. After a measured number of steps, he stopped and turned to his right, staring at a particular place on the south wall of the tunnel.

"According to the map," he said, "the ✠ marks a spot five or six feet inside this wall. It might be more or it might be less. It might even be five or six feet on either side, but this is where it shows on the map. If there's gold or anything else buried under that ✠ we're going to find it here."

"Bring down as many five gallon plastic buckets as you can from outside," he said abruptly in a tone of voice that demanded full and immediate compliance.

In a matter of minutes, we were standing in the middle of a pile of fifteen or twenty buckets.

"That should be more than enough for now," he said.

"Well, Bruce," Dick said, "you're the younger man and an archaeologist to boot. I'll give you the privilege of digging if you want to take it."

Without another word, Bruce grabbed a small pickaxe, attached to his belt like a hunting knife, and started carefully hacking into the tunnel wall. After one or two hacks, he took a garden trowel and carefully scooped the loose dirt into one of the buckets.

I looked at my watch and figured, at this rate, it would take him two or three hours to dig out five feet of dirt.

"Can you dig any faster?" I asked.

It was a rude question and completely inappropriate but before I could apologize Bruce answered by saying, "Yes, I believe I can."

He explained the dirt seemed unusually soft and he could just as easily dig it out with a spade. The buckets filled up quickly as he dug, and we kept busy carrying the heavy, full ones out of the way and replacing them with empties.

About four feet in, Bruce stopped digging.

He leaned the shovel on the wall behind him and pulled a small whiskbroom out of his pocket. With a particular care that can only come from years of experience, he gently brushed a small amount of soil from a spot level with the tunnel floor.

"It's a bone," he said. "I can't tell for sure, but it looks like part of the hand and wrist of a child."

Dick, who was wearing a hat reminiscent of Indiana Jones, removed it and placed it over his heart.

"I'm not sure I want to dig any more right now," Bruce sighed. "I don't want to disturb this more than necessary. This kind of excavation needs to be done very carefully and I don't have the tools for it with me at the moment."

"I guess that was what the ⚓ was for," Mona suggested.

"But what about the buried gold?" Connie said in a voice that betrayed disappointment.

Robert, who had been standing in the back with Joe and Chia, stepped forward and pointed at something two or three feet above where the bone had been found.

What Robert pointed at was a small projection of dirt that should have fallen off by its own weight. Something was holding it in place in defiance of the law of gravity.

"What's this?" Robert asked.

"I don't know," Bruce said thoughtfully. "I was looking down and didn't even notice it. Let's take a look see."

He brushed it gently with his whisk. In the light cast by the line of small bulbs the police had stretched along the ceiling of the tunnel, it gleamed like gold.

Bruce stepped back in silence, while Dick and Sonja quietly said, "I'll be damned" at the same time.

"What is it?" asked Chia, who had followed Robert to where she could see things better.

"Is it gold?" Connie asked, hopefully.

"I'm not sure," Bruce answered, "but it doesn't look like gold. It looks more like copper. It's duller—

and there, do you see it? There's a hint of green on the edge."

He began to brush away more of the dirt and slowly exposed what looked like a small, flat sheet of copper. When it came time to extract it he carefully put on a pair of soft, cotton gloves and pulled it free.

"There are words on it," he said as he blew off the dust and knocked off the small amount of dirt that had adhered to it.

The tunnel was as quiet as the sound of a baby's breath.

"What does it say?" Mona whispered, as if she was the only one who had thought of the question.

"The letters are scratched into the copper but they are written in a beautiful script and etched more deeply into the metal than I would have expected. Here, if I put it at an angle to the light I can see it quite well.

He read the words slowly and in a tone of voice that would have seemed reverent even in a place of worship. As he read, the words transformed the tunnel into a holy place, a temple of history, the house of God.

Never had I felt God's presence more powerfully than I did at that moment. Not in St. Peter's in Rome, not in Notre Dame in Paris, not even in the depths of despair when my life had been hanging in the balance.

Here lie the mortal remains of Goldie Johnson,
A child born a slave but who died free.
Now she is free forever.
September 18, 1857.

As we stood in awed silence, the letters written on the map made sense for the first time.

"gld" they said, "bried hre"

It wasn't gold that had been buried, it was a little girl named Goldie.

Our greed and lust for treasure had turned into dust and shame.

Sonja started sobbing and it was Connie who stepped up to console her . . . and to be consoled herself.

Chia made the sign of the cross on her chest and Joe started backing up as if he had seen a ghost.

I realized my heart was pounding like a pile driver. I was tense as steel but I began to relax when I felt the gentle touch of Mona's arm around my waist.

"I think I've seen enough," Robert said. "I'm going outside for some air."

Silently we all agreed with Robert, and silently we all climbed the ladder and emerged into the life-giving light of early afternoon.

We were standing in a place where over 150 years ago, a drama of life and death had played out in the midst of a tragic conflict between freedom and slavery. Heroes without names had walked here and at least one of them had died and been buried with tender and respectful love.

All human life should be worthy of such respect, I thought to myself. *How sad that the world has made so little progress over the centuries. Are we any more respectful of human life now than we were then? . . . a time when men, women and children could be owned and regarded as objects to be used or abused at the whim of their masters?*

I realized the thought was profound even as I pondered it. I wasn't even sure where the thought came from. It was deeper than I usually get when it comes to . . . to things that are as important as life and death . . . and other things that really matter.

In the tunnel, I had felt the presence of God, an experience that was like a soul-shaking explosion of power, love and eternity rolled into one. The moment changed me somehow and, for the first time, I began to understand some of what Mona has been trying to explain to me since we first met.

I turned to her and held her in as tight an embrace as I could without hurting her arm. With her free hand, she returned it.

The silence continued for a moment until it was broken by Joe saying, "I'm hungry, let's eat!"

Officer Inouye assigned a junior officer to stand watch and joined the two professors and the rest of us on a pilgrimage to Bargain Burgers for a celebration of life, liberty, and lunch.

When 2:00 p.m. came along, it was time to head home.

The professors handed the stolen journal pages back to Sonja and in return, Connie presented them with the photocopied pages she had gotten from the library.

"Sonja and I can get more copies if we need them," Connie said, turning to Sonja as she said added, "and I can't wait to read your thesis if you ever get it written!"

Sonja laughed.

"Unless I get thrown out of the program for what happened this week, I'm going to have to rethink the whole project, but even if the revisions set me back another twelve months, it will be worth it."

There were hugs all around and promises to hold a reunion in Albany some day. Then the adventure was over . . . at least for the seven of us.

Connie and Joe hopped into the Miata and headed back to Hartford to reclaim Connie's car; Sonja climbed onto her bike, all girded up in helmet and leather; and Robert, Chia, Mona and I squished into Sid's car. Chia drove, Robert sat next to her and Mona and I took on the duties of being back-seat drivers on the trip home to Manhattan.

As we pulled out of the parking lot, Mona turned her head for one final look at the sinkhole and vacant lot that had shaped our lives over the past few days.

"I don't know if I want to come back here, again," she said. "It doesn't make a whole lot of sense to waste more time and money just so I can relive a nightmare."

"The burgers were good, though," I said.

"That's true," she replied.

"We could always do drive-thru," Robert added as an afterthought.

When she looked back, Mona had seen something that didn't register in her mind until later. It was like it says in Mona's Bible; "they may look but not see."

Mona didn't have to wait long, however, before she remembered what she had seen when she looked.

Before we got onto the Interstate Chia stopped to get gas. As we slowed to turn across traffic into a service station, Mona fulfilled her responsibility as a back-seat driver by turning her head to check the cars behind us.

"That's strange," she said. "The car behind us started their turn signal just after Chia did."

"What's so strange about that?" Chia asked as she waited for the oncoming traffic to go by.

"Because I saw the same car pull out of the Bargain Burger parking lot when we left . . . at least I think it was the same car. Most black sedans look the same, but this one has tinted windows that are really dark."

"It's probably just a coincidence," I suggested, trying to help Mona avoid a head-on collision with paranoia.

Mona's suspicions got another boost when the black car backed into a parking place instead of pulling up to the gas pump. This wouldn't have been a big deal either, except no one got out of the car.

"Don't stare," Mona said. "They parked so they can see everything we do."

"Sure, okay," I said. "I'll check the oil. Chia, pop the hood for me."

"What are you doing?" Mona said.

"I'm going to take a peek at our friends without staring at them."

I placed myself in a position in front of the hood where I could appear to be checking the engine while getting a good look at the car parked behind us. In the front seat were two men. Both were of average height. Both were clean-shaven and neither of them looked as if they were particularly interested in staring back at me. Something moved in the back seat so I assumed there was at least one person there as well but, like Mona said, the dark tinting made it almost impossible to see inside.

"It doesn't look too suspicious to me," said when I got back in the car. "Just two or three guys taking a rest break. Maybe when they saw us turning they decided they might as well stop, too, before hitting the on-ramp. Maybe the driver had to make a phone call or who knows what. There's no reason to get all paranoid about it."

"Are you saying I'm paranoid?" Mona glared as she slid herself as far away from me as possible without removing her seat belt.

I started to say, "No, of course not," but I realized I *had* implied she was paranoid by saying she shouldn't be.

"I'm sorry," I said. "I didn't mean to imply you were paranoid."

The truth was, of course, that I *had* meant to imply it, and when I said, "I'm sorry," I lied.

I suppose I shouldn't have been surprised that Mona was still jittery from what she had gone through. All of us, including me, were still shaking inside, but I had been through it before and knew that the best way to handle it was to let it go and move on so it wouldn't take control of my life.

As Chia pulled back into traffic and merged onto the Interstate Mona said, "The black car pulled out when we did and is three or four cars behind us."

"Slow down a little," Robert said, "and let the cars in between go past."

In a few seconds, there was nothing but air between us.

Robert's a big man so it was no easy thing for him to turn his head around far enough to look out the back window, but he did.

"The guy on the left looks like Doc," he said, "but he's wearing dark classes so it's hard to be sure. If the other two are Bombo and Sam, that would make Sam the driver with Bombo in the back. He'd be too short to see easily."

"Yes," I said, "nice theory, but the driver doesn't have a beard."

"It's easy to cut off a beard," Chia said.

Suddenly, everyone in the car was paranoid except me.

"Suppose you've got it right and the car is filled with bad guys, what are we supposed to do about it?"

No one offered an answer but as it turned out, we got one anyway.

We were approaching the interchange near Catskill when the black car accelerated, pulled alongside us and slammed into the side of our car. Chia hit the brakes and turned the wheel, trying to push back, but the other car was bigger and heavier. It hit us hard enough to force us onto the guardrail. At sixty miles an hour the right side of the car lifted off the ground and for one deathly moment, I thought we were going to flip over the railing and disintegrate down the embankment on the other side.

As if by a miracle the moment passed, the black car passed and Mona passed out. There was no miracle in her passing out, though, because she had hit her head against the side window and put a crack in it. She was out cold, possibly with a crack in her head that matched the one in the window.

I was dialing 911 when Robert said, "You're not paranoid when someone actually _is_ trying to kill you."

Robert was right, of course, and I had been wrong . . . very, very wrong.

Mona regained consciousness almost immediately and in a matter of minutes the EMTs arrived. They put her neck in a brace, lifted her onto a gurney and slid her into the back of an ambulance. Sid's car was totaled but the rest of us had only been shaken up.

Chia stayed with the car to give her report to the state troopers and to wait for a tow truck to haul the wreck away. Robert stayed with her, of course, but I hitched a ride in the ambulance to be with Mona.

The black car didn't have a license plate on the front and the collision happened so fast none of us had a chance to see if there was one in the back. All we knew was the blue pickup had morphed into a black sedan and three of the Four Horsemen of the Apocalypse were determined to finish us off.

I mentioned this to Mona during the ride to the hospital and she explained, "The first three horsemen are war, famine, and death. You got lucky with the metaphor. Whether you knew it or not I think you got it right."

"Who's the fourth one?"

"He's someone with a crown riding a white horse and no one knows for sure, but it might be Jesus, returning in power, wrath and judgment. Then again . . . ."

It was good to see that Mona's brain was still working but I would have been even happier if I had seen Jesus riding along next to us on a horse.

X-rays showed Mona's head hadn't been Humpty-Dumpty-ed but she was diagnosed with a concussion. It took the rest of the afternoon to sort everything out. There was the matter of criminal assault with a deadly weapon, the fact we were driving someone else's car and reports that had to be written by the state troopers and local police. Calls were made to Albany and an all-points-bulletin was issued for the state.

Chapter Twenty

Wake Up Mona
Friday Evening

Mona was released from the ER in time for dinner and Robert managed to pick up a one-way rental car from a company that wasn't called Speedy's. The way Robert said the words "one way rental" triggered the thought that maybe the car was programmed to only drive in only one direction. That was fine with me because I only wanted to go in one direction anyway—home.

Because it was getting late, we drove through a fast food place and picked up tacos and burritos. Mona ordered a quesadilla and ate less than half of it before she fell asleep.

"Wake her up," Robert said. "If she has a concussion we need to keep her awake so we can tell what's going on."

"Wake up, Mona," I said. "I'm feeling lonely already."

"Then move in with Aunt Lucille," she mumbled before falling asleep again.

"She sounds delirious," I said.

Chia pulled off at the next interchange, gave Robert the car keys, moved me up to First Class and stepped into the Rumble Seat with Mona. Girls like to talk more than guys so Chia was able to keep the conversation going until Robert dropped us off in front of our apartment building two hours later.

My first concern, of course, was Mona.

My second concern was telling Sid his car had been totaled.

The ER doc told Mona to take some ibuprofen for pain if she had any. Since she was already taking it for the pain in her arm, she was all set from the get-go.

Once we were inside, Mona sat down on the sofa and slept as still and quiet as a corpse except for the breathing, the heart beating and things like that. On the other hand, I couldn't sleep at all. I felt tense, nervous and, although it was embarrassing to admit it, I felt a little paranoid. After all, there were three horsemen who seemed determined to smite us and as far as I could tell there was no Jesus in sight.

Chapter Twenty-One

Blizzard

Saturday Morning

I suppose it didn't matter that I didn't sleep well during the night, because the phone woke me a 4:30 a.m. anyway. It was London calling with an update on the Rembrandt painting. Whoever dialed my number must not have been aware New York City was in a time zone where the sun hadn't come up yet.

"Is this Mr. Maurison?"

"Yes," I said, "at least I was when I went to bed last night. Do you know what time it is in New York?"

"Why, yes I do. It is 4:30 in the morning. I'm sorry if I woke you up. I get up around 3:30 a.m. myself, but that isn't important. Why I'm calling is because something new has come up regarding the

Rembrandt the National Gallery is holding on your behalf."

"That's all very nice," I said, "but who are you?"

"Please accept my sincere apology," the voice replied with a stiff upper lip. "I suppose I was carried away by the excitement. Allow me to introduce myself. I'm Robert Townsend-Smythe. I am a member of the committee that recently authenticated your painting as a genuine Rembrandt self-portrait."

"Glad to meet you," I yawned, not sure whether I should hang up or hang in to see what the excitement was all about. I knew if I hung up Smythe would call me back later. Pushing the "Pause" button now might be worth an extra hour of sleep, but, as usual, curiosity got the best of me.

"Go ahead," I said. "If it's good news I might as well get excited about it, too."

"I'm not sure we mentioned this before. If we didn't, it was because it was so obvious we assumed you and everyone else already knew about it . . . ."

"Is there a point to this?" I yawned again. "If there is, I'd like to hear it."

"What is it, Mike? Who's on the phone?"

It was Mona. She had been so deep in Never-Land she hadn't heard the phone ring. Smythe was already talking again so I put one hand behind my ear, whispered, "Listen," and hit the "Speaker" icon on my phone.

"Mr. Maurison, do you remember the number that was written on the back of the canvas?"

"No, not really, I don't remember seeing a number. I didn't spend much time looking at the back of the painting anyway, except when it was rolled up. Why? What about the number?"

"I can't believe you didn't notice it. I admit it has become quite faint over the years but it showed up quite well under infra-red light."

"Maybe if I'd called in Superman as a consultant I might have known about it," I said, oozing with sarcasm.

"Superman? Why Superman?"

"Because he has x-ray vision," I explained.

"Oh, that wouldn't have helped at all. We tried that right away. It was very helpful but it didn't highlight the number on the back."

I considered the possibility that Mr. Smythe had never read a comic book or gone to a movie in his life.

"The number," Smyth explained, "was '27,' written in an old style with the usual cross line through the seven. It's presence on the back of the painting baffled us for quite a while until tests concluded it was 18th century in origin."

"Let me guess," I said as I stifled yet another yawn. "Does this have something to do with you being excited?"

"Why yes, it does," he said, missing my sarcasm for a second time in a row. "Once we had determined it was French, Benson recalled another painting with a similar number written on the back. He had never seen it himself but he had heard about it some years ago at an art symposium."

I had no idea what he was talking about; I had no idea who Benson was; and I had no idea how anyone could tell that a number had been written in French; so of course I said, "Have you come to the point, yet?"

"Almost there," he said cheerily. "The symposium topic concerned a French noble in the 18th century who acquired a number of paintings he had carefully catalogued by number. Unfortunately, the paintings were lost when his chateau burned while being looted during the French Revolution. No trace of the noble or his family survived and the records seem to suggest some of them may have lost their heads, as was the custom in those days. The art was lost but somehow the catalogue survived.

"Let me guess," I interrupted. "The painting mentioned at the seminar matched the name and number of one of the paintings on the guy's inventory list, and the number on that painting had been written in a way similar to the one on the back of my painting, so you think my Rembrandt was part of the guy's collection."

There was a very long pause but since I wasn't going anywhere I was happy to wait.

"Mike," Mona whispered. "Stop showing off. Shut up and let the man talk."

"I'm just trying to move the conversation along," I whispered back.

"Why yes," Smythe eventually replied. "That is exactly right. Well done! You should be a detective or an inspector of some kind. You would be very good at it, I should think."

I was tempted, but because of Mona, I bit my tongue a little, but not enough to make it bleed.

"The noble, whose title was the Marquis De Chauve, listed thirty-two artworks in his collection. The only painting ever recovered was the one discussed at the seminar. It was numbered '12' and was listed on the Marquis' list along with the title, the artist's name, and the year it had been painted."

"What about number 27?" I asked, trying to skip ahead to the last page of the whodunit.

"That's the curious part. The inventory listed it only as a 'Self Portrait.' The name of the artist was not recorded, possibly because Rembrandt's initials hadn't been put on the painting yet. It's quite possible the Marquis added the signature himself. He undoubtedly believed it was by Rembrandt and, because of that, didn't feel he was being dishonest by putting the artist's name on it. For him it must have seemed no different than the way we feel about putting labels on museum walls today."

" . . . and so . . . ?" I asked.

" . . . and so . . . now we have at least a partial provenance for the painting. Painting number '12' came to light after an antique dealer purchased it as part of an estate sale. The painting was wrapped in cloth dating to the early 19th century and was still sealed in a wooden crate from the same period. It's possible the family who owned it had never opened the crate or seen the painting since it came into their possession."

"So," I asked, suddenly sensing we were getting close to the point, "who claimed ownership of the painting?"

"When it was discovered the painting was valuable, the family who sold it tried to sue to get it back, arguing it had not been a part of the sale and the dealer had taken it by mistake. The court ruled in favor of the antique dealer, giving the opinion that, since he bought it, he owned it."

"So," I asked, "who owns my painting?"

"We still don't know, but its provenance suggests it may have been a part of the same estate that owned number '12.' It doesn't seem to have been stolen by Nazis during the war, but it does seem to have been stolen from someone . . . somewhere . . . perhaps very recently. The police or whoever takes charge of these things will advertise its existence and if no one claims it, you will probably get to keep it . . . unless, of course, the person who owned it or the people who put it in the dumpster step forward and say it's theirs.

"If you want my opinion, I think, like the other painting, your Rembrandt had been an unknown part of an estate. Somehow, someone saw it and guessed its value but rather than drawing attention to it by making an offer, they arranged to steal it.

"Now, for obvious reasons, they can't claim it and the person they stole it from probably isn't aware they ever owned it. Unless the thieves incriminate themselves by revealing where they got it, it will probably be yours. 'Finder's keepers,' as they say. Wouldn't it be a kick if that's how it plays out?"

"But you could be wrong, right?" I added as a caveat.

"You're right," he said, reversing the word order, "I could be wrong."

That, as it turned out, was the gist of what he had spent twenty minutes trying to say—"I might be right or I might be wrong."

Wonderful.

"Mona," I said when the call was over, "I don't think I'll get excited until someone decides it's ours. Until then, the $30 million is no more real to me than the buried gold we thought we found on the map . . . ."

" . . . except, "Mona said, "we've actually seen the painting and know where it is. In any case, it's agreed: We won't spend any of it unless we have it in our hands."

"Agreed," I said. "Until then, I'm content with being poor, because as long as I have you, I'm richer than a Rembrandt."

We kissed, we felt giddy, and when that was over, we fell back to sleep for an hour.

At 6:00 a.m., my phone rang again. This time it was a local call from someone who should have been able to look out his window and see the sun hadn't come all the way up yet. It was "Sweet Spot" William.

"Mr. Maurison. I am a patient man but I do not suffer fools gladly. Unless you provide the evidence I need by four o'clock this afternoon, you can kiss your contract good-bye. I hope to hear from you soon. Any last words? . . . I didn't think so. Good-bye, Mr. Maurison."

It's quite interesting how one phone call saying you might be getting a check in the mail for $30 million can put you to sleep while another one saying you might be losing out on a job worth $1,000 can snap you wide awake.

I was wide-awake enough to remember that Mona and I really needed that $1,000 . . . especially since Mona had missed three days pay and I had been chasing gold dust for the past week instead of bringing home the cured pork. Even my credit card was looking thinner.

When I looked across the room Mona was still pretending to be one of the living dead so I got dressed as quietly as I could.

Mona, I wrote on a scrap of paper, *I've got something to do that can't wait. I hope your arm and head feel better today. Love, Mike.*

As Mona trained me to do, I stuck the note onto the refrigerator under the "I ❤ NY" magnet and shut the apartment door quietly behind me as I left.

I hadn't even reached the ground floor of the building when my phone rang again.

It was my friend Sid.

"Hi, Sid," I said. "Isn't 6:20 in the morning a bit early for you on a Saturday?"

"Mike, I just got up to go to the bathroom and checked my email. What does this mean, *'Dear Sid, I owe you a car. Mike'* . . . Well?"

"It means your car is DOA in the morgue up in Catskill."

"You killed it?"

"Someone else did when they broadsided us on the Interstate yesterday afternoon. It was a murder, not a suicide."

"Is everyone okay? I mean, I loaned the car to Mona, is she alright?"

"Just a small concussion. You heard about us on the news, right?"

"Yes, of course I did. Didn't you get my texts and phone messages?"

"Sid, nothing personal, but yesterday when I got my phone back from the police, so many emails, messages and texts came up that I haven't even looked through them yet. Every media outlet on the East Coast is trying to get me and Mona to go on their show or be interviewed for something. There's so much spam I'm tempted to delete everything and start my phone life all over from scratch."

"Mike, there's something I was going to tell you about the car."

"What was that?"

"My company just bought me a new one so I was planning to give the old one to you as a gift."

"Oh," I said. "Thanks . . . I'm deeply touched . . . really."

"Don't mention it. I signed the registration into your name two days ago. She's all yours!"

As usual, my timing was perfect.

"Sid?"

"Yes, Mike?"

"If I . . . you know . . . if I ever need to borrow a car for some reason . . . ."

"I'm listening . . . ."

" . . . do you suppose I might be able to borrow your new car once in a while . . . you know . . . when you aren't using it?"

There was a brief moment of silence followed by what sounded like uncontrollable laughter.

"Mike," Sid said, choking for breath, "you are one of a kind, you know that? But you're a good kind of weird, so, 'Yes,' I'll give you the key to my new car. Feel free to use it like the one you led to the slaughter yesterday."

"Does this mean I get to keep whatever the old car's worth for scrap?"

"It's all yours."

"And if there's any insurance money for the car?"

"That's all yours, too . . . if you have insurance."

"Why in the world would I have auto insurance when I didn't even know I owned a car until two minutes ago? By the way, how are the kids?"

"Just fine. They really like the new car smell and want me to drive their friends everywhere so they can show off. Children are a lot like new car smells. The older they get, the less you can find them and then, all of a sudden, they've moved out and they're gone."

"Until you buy a new one," I said.

Sid laughed again and said, "Let me know when you can stop by and pick up the key. I've already had a spare made for you."

In Manhattan, there are good, generous people like Sid standing on every street corner. It's kinda cool, though, when you actually have one of them as a friend.

"How about if I pick up the key now?" I said. "I've got to get over to Brooklyn this morning. I was going to rent a car but you'll get a free tank of gas if you'll let me borrow yours."

"It's all yours, Mike, but I've got to warn you, the tank is full and the car gets 35 mpg. I don't think you'll be spending much on gas!"

There's no doubt about it—I've got the best friends in the world.

During Sid's call, I sat on the bottom step of the stairway. When it was over, I stood up, walked towards the front door, and stopped again.

It occurred to me that I had absolutely no idea what I was going to do or why. When I told Sid I was going to drive to Brooklyn I was thinking I might discover who the real Leslie McGillicutty was and take it from there. Now I couldn't see any reason to waste my time with it. After all, it wasn't Mr. Leslie who was important. I already knew his connection with "Royal Throne" and since William had already told me he was a he, I didn't need to travel to Brooklyn to figure out his wife or girl friend was in cahoots with him.

What I needed to do was trace him back to someone at Royal Throne. I suppose I could have knocked on Leslie's door and asked if he had a handwritten note signed by the owner of Royal

Throne contracting him to destroy every Sweet Spot toilet in Manhattan, but that idea wasn't going to go anywhere.

I could also bust into his house and rummage through his stuff looking for a smoking gun but that would probably get me three to five years in the state pen.

If there was a weak link anywhere, it would have to be someone at the company office or someone at the construction site. Since both places were just south of where I was standing I decided I didn't need to borrow Sid's car after all.

Once again I had been compulsive, but this time I reeled myself in before I was pulled out of the boat by one of my imaginative figments.

I headed for the construction site first because it was within walking distance. I'd forgotten it was Saturday and when I got there the place was shut down as tight as a hatch on a submarine.

I guessed there had to be a security guard on site somewhere so I stood by the entry gate and waited for him or her to come past on his or her rounds. I didn't have to wait long. In two minutes, I was gesturing her over to the gate.

In my pocket was the small digital recorder that I use for moments like this. I switched it on.

"What do you want," she asked as if she was James Cagney about to shove a grapefruit in my face.

With today's emphasis on gender equality, being a guy doesn't seem to matter much anymore. You can see the role reversal all the time in television ads and the movies, but now I was seeing it through a construction gate where the king of the castle was a girl.

"What I want," I said, "Is to talk to the person in charge of the site."

"That's who you're talking to now."

"In that case I need to tell you that at 1:00 p.m. I'm coming through the gate with a key."

I held up the key I use to unlock the desk drawer in my office.

"Are you crazy?" the guard said with her volume turned up a tad too high for the occasion. "That's in broad daylight!"

There was a pause, as she looked me over more carefully.

"Who are you, anyway? And what happened to your face?" she asked with the volume turned down a notch.

"I ran into a fist. The other guy's in jail so I guess I won. Who sent me? Mr. L.M. sent me to cover for him today. He's given me the tools I need to do the job. Three minutes is all I'll need. I'll be on time so you won't even need to miss your rounds."

"Mr. L.M.? . . . Oh, you mean Leslie, but why would *he* send you? He's not the boss. I can't let you in unless the boss says it's okay."

240

"Look," I said. "I don't know anything about a boss, and like I said I'm only covering for Leslie because his wife crashed their truck last night and broke her arm. If I need permission from somebody, who do I get it from? I don't want to get anybody into trouble, especially me."

"Sorry, Mr. . . . what did you say your name was again?"

"I didn't and I'm not going to, either. Now listen, if I don't do the work today Leslie's going to be in hot water. Someone really wants to send a message by doing this in the middle of the day and today's the day because there aren't workers hovering around like vultures searching for road kill."

"You'll have to talk to Gene about it," she said, "and I didn't tell you anything, *capiche*?"

"Yeah, sure," I said, not intimidated by the implied threat. "Who the hell is Gene?"

"If you don't know then get lost . . . or ask Mr. L.M. or whatever you call him. You can go stick your head in a toilet, for all I care. Do what you have to do and leave me out of it."

She turned to walk away but stopped as if she was reconsidering something. Then she turned and walked back to the gate.

"In case you need to know, I clock in at this station every ten minutes starting at the top of the hour."

241

She stared me straight in the eye. When neither of us blinked she turned away again, but this time she kept walking. I knew the timing of her rounds already but it was gratifying to see my BS was smooth enough to get her to squeal.

I reached in my pocket and turned the recorder off.

So, the fix is in after all and everybody seems to know about it, I said in consultation with myself. *Now all I've got to do is find out who Gene is.*

My next stop was the Royal Throne office. It was too far to walk so I took a cab.

When I paid off the driver and walked to the gate, there was a sign: "Closed Saturday and Sunday."

I looked at my watch. It was 10:00 a.m. and I had until 4:00 p.m. to give William the gift that keeps on giving. At this point in the game, I might have been stumped if it weren't for the words printed in small letters at the bottom of the sign: "For after-hour assistance please call 555-7710."

With nothing better to do, I turned on my pocket recorder and held it next to my phone while I dialed the number. What I got was an answering machine.

Thank you for calling Royal Throne Portable Toilets. We are unable to answer your call but we understand your message is important. Please leave your name, your phone number

*and your message after the beep. We will do
our best to return your call as soon as possible.
Remember—With Royal Throne You'll Be
flushed With Pride!"*

I didn't have a message to leave but out of habit I
punched the "o" on my keypad, just in case there
was an operator wasting the day away waiting for
me to call.

To my surprise, there was.

"This is Trudy, may I help you?"

For the second time that morning, I had
absolutely no I idea what I was doing, but I did my
best to ad-lib like a comedian at the Improv.

"Thank you, Trudy, it's good to talk with you
again. Sometime we'll have to get together for coffee
so I can attach a face to the dulcet tone of your
voice."

"Whoever you are you're full of it, and wherever
you are it must still be winter, because you're
snowing like a blizzard. Now how can I help you?"

"Don't take it personally, Trudy, but I actually
called to talk with Gene. Can you connect me, or
transfer me, or tell me how I can get in touch with
him? I'm returning his call and he left a message
saying it was important, but he didn't leave a
number."

I was piling it on so deep I wouldn't have been
surprised to learn the weather service was preparing

to issue a winter storm warning for the area around the Royal Throne office.

"Mr. Handel isn't in the office today but I'll let him know you called. Please tell me your name and a number where we can return you call."

Handel? What a name for a toilet company executive to have! I tried not to laugh out loud, but even though I knew he had to be a calloused jerk I still felt sorry for him being stuck with "Royal Throne Toilet-Handel" printed on his business card.

After swallowing the laugh, I said, "Gene wouldn't want me to, you know, say anything to anyone about this or to leave a message, even with you. I'm sure you're trustworthy and probably have a surgically-implanted zip-lock on your lips, but I have to talk to Gene personally."

If I didn't start shoveling now, the drifts were going to get so deep I'd have to rent a plow to get back to my apartment.

I could hear Trudy give a soft sigh before saying, "This might get me fired but I'll ring him up and ask if he wants to take your call. Who should I say is calling."

"Just tell him it's Leslie."

There was a long pause. I was convinced Trudy knew McGillicutty well enough to notice that my voice and his didn't match up, but, as it turned out, I needn't have worried. The pause was because I had been put on hold and Trudy didn't have elevator music on her machine.

"Hello?" came a man's voice. "Who is this?"

"Leslie."

"Leslie who?"

The conversation had just started and already it was degenerating into a knock-knock joke.

"The guy with the four-inch drill bit," I answered. "Is this Gene?"

His voice crunched down into a whispering croak.

"Who else would it be . . . and what the . . . ."

He stopped in mid-sentence, probably so his mother's ears wouldn't turn red.

"Don't ever phone me here again. What's wrong with you?"

People had been asking me that exact same question all week and I still didn't have a good answer for it.

"Someone left me a message to do a job in broad daylight," I said. "I'm supposed to hit the same Sweet Spot toilets I hit at the parking garage site earlier this week. Who's jerking me around on this? I'm not going out there at 1:00 in the afternoon even if the workers are off for the day. It'd be suicide."

"No one's asking you to fall on your sword," Gene said with his voice falling to a low rumble. "I didn't approve it and I don't know who did.

245

Something's full of crap and it's not one of my toilets!"

"So," I said, "I guess I get the day off and 'Sweet William' gets off the hook. Whatever you say boss. I'm sorry I called. I won't do it again."

"No . . . you were right to call. There would have been shit flying if you'd gone ahead and done it this afternoon. Just lay low for a while until I figure out what happened . . . and don't do anything unless you hear the word, "manure" somewhere in the message. Got it?"

"Got it," I said, and pushed the "End Call" button on my phone.

I held up the digital recorder and added the date, the time, and the phone numbers I had dialed. Then I turned it off and put it back in my pocket.

At that point, the sun came out and the snow began to melt as if it was summer—which, of course, it was.

I knew that what I had done wasn't completely kosher, but even though it couldn't be admitted as evidence in a court of law, it was good enough to get me a payday from "Sweet Spot William." Once I handed him the recording, it would be up to him to figure out what to do with it.

It had been a good day's work and it was still only 10:30 in the morning.

I took a cab back to the apartment. After letting myself in and looking around I couldn't find Mona anywhere. When she returned from an errand a few minutes later, she found me sound asleep on the sofa.

Chapter Twenty-Two

Pearl Onions & Peas
Saturday Afternoon

I awoke to the sound of laughter.

Mona was in the kitchen trying to fix tuna sandwiches for lunch, and she was laughing so hard tears were running down her cheeks.

"Doesn't that hurt?" I asked.

"Does what hurt?"

"Your head . . . when you laugh?"

"Why should my head hurt when I laugh?"

"Because you have a concussion, that's why. When someone has a concussion and their blood pressure goes up, their head hurts. Laughing makes a person's blood pressure go up, so your head should be hurting."

"Then I guess I don't have a concussion after all. That's a good thing, don't you think?"

"It's a very good thing, but what's so funny?"

One look at the kitchen answered my question.

Since one arm was in a cast, Mona had tried to open a can of tuna with one hand. There was tuna oil everywhere.

Next, she tried to mix it in a bowl with mayonnaise and pickle relish with one hand. There were bits of relish and tuna mixed with mayonnaise everywhere.

Finally, she tried to spread the mix onto a slice of bread with one hand. The knife stuck to the bread. The bread was now on the floor, face down— and that's why Mona was laughing.

The scene reminded me of a lady I once knew named Barbara. Barbara had suffered from cancer and had surgery to remove one of her arms at the shoulder. She was completely cured of the cancer and went south to Florida for a month every winter to keep warm.

"What do you do when you're down there?" I asked.

"Oh," she said, "I visit my friends, I go on long walks and I go swimming every morning."

"Barbara, excuse me for asking, but when you swim, don't you just go around in circles? How can you swim in a straight line with one arm?"

She laughed almost as loud as Mona had laughed.

"You're right," she smiled. "It took me a long time to learn how to swim again, but now I'm pretty good at it. If you want, we can go over to the "Y" and I'll race you!"

I turned down the offer partially because Barbara was eighty years old, but mostly because I would have been embarrassed when I came in second.

"Mona," I said, "by the time you learn how to fix a tuna sandwich with one hand you'll be all healed up and won't need to do it again anyway, so why waste your time . . . and the tuna?"

"Because it's there," she smiled.

"Well said, Mrs. Mallory," I replied.

"It was *Mister* Mallory who said it," Mona corrected me.

After a short pause she added, "I'm not sure if there even *was* a Mrs. Mallory."

"If there *was* a Mrs. Mallory, she could never have been as brave and as beautiful as you are," I said, as I bent over and began wiping up the floor.

"Let's eat out for lunch," Mona announced, "I don't feel like tuna anymore."

"Just a second," I said as I stepped over to Mona's laptop and downloaded my digital recording onto a flash drive.

When I finished, I tucked it away in my pocket, took Mona's hand and led her out the door.

As we walked to Neil's Coffee Shop, Mona turned to me and said, "Mike, does it bother you to think how awful you must look to everyone who sees you?"

"No," I said, "as long as there isn't a mirror in front of me I'm fine with it. Does it bother you?"

"Not at all. You're a hero and that's your badge of honor. If I were you I'd be proud to wear it."

"I'd rather have a medal," I said.

To my surprise, Mona didn't order the Swiss steak.

"I'll have a burger and fries," she said, "in memory of the good times we had at Bargain Burgers."

"I'll have a bowl of chili and a cola," I said, "in memory of the good time we're having at Neil's right now."

"*Touché*," Mona replied. "In that case, I'll have the Swiss steak."

Me and my big mouth.

While we waited for the food, I phoned Sid and apologized for not showing up to get the key to his car.

"Don't sweat it," he said. "The kids have a tent set up in the living room and we're standing in the kitchen holding our hands over the stove, pretending we're boiling hot dogs over a campfire. It's a good day. Hope yours is, too."

I started to say something to Mona about how much Sid seems to enjoy his kids and maybe we should think about if or when we might want to start thinking about it, too.

Being a parent has been a touchy subject for me even before I met Mona. Until recently, I figured children were something other people had, but then I met Mona's parents and realized if they hadn't had Mona I wouldn't have had Mona either, so having kids might not be such a bad thing after all.

I started to say it, but when the waitress interrupted us to put our lunch on the table I decided to tuck the thought away and save it for later.

"What's the deal?" I said as we started munching. "You're eating your peas. I've never seen you eat the peas before."

"Now you have," she said. "I never realized how good they taste with the pearl onions. Unless you try something you'll never know if you're going to like it or not."

"Like treasure hunting?" I suggested.

"Actually," she said with a smile that would have hurt my face if I had tried it, "I was thinking of marriage. You see, until I met you, marriage was like peas. I didn't want to try it but I wanted all the things that went with it. Because of you, I decided I'd give it a try and, just like the peas, it was better than I thought it would be."

"If I'm the peas," I asked, "then who are the onions?"

"Our friends, of course."

"And who's the Swiss steak?"

"God," she said as she stuffed the last of the peas in her mouth.

"God?" I asked.

"God," she said

"Here," she added, sticking her fork into a piece of steak and shoving it in my mouth. "Try it. It's good."

Mona was right. The steak was good.

"Here's a Bible verse," she said with her mouth full of God. "It's from Psalms, but I can't remember which one. It goes like this: 'Taste and see that the Lord is good.'"

"I get it," I said. "It's sort of like the old commercial where one kid says, 'Try it, Mikey' and after he takes a bite they say, 'Mikey likes it!' and then they eat it too."

"Yep," Mona said. "That's how it's been with me and God. 'Try it, you'll like it.'"

That's all she said . . . which was a good thing, because if she'd pushed the point much further I might have come down with indigestion.

As I nibbled on the last soda cracker, I thought about the times God had shown up in my life during the past week. I had no idea why God had suddenly decided to take aim at me like a sniper, but God's aim was true and my heart had been hit more than once.

I hadn't spent much time thinking about God until I met Mona, and even then I did my best to stay as far away from him as possible. When I first went to church as a favor to her, I went for the music, but what I found was something that seemed to be real—at least to the people who took the time and effort to get up, get dressed and get to church on time every week. God seemed to be real to Mona and Pastor Cheryl, too. What God had to say about right and wrong and sin and forgiveness had all made sense. Maybe the saying is wrong , , , maybe you *can* have your steak and eat it, too.

None of it has turned me into anything worse than I was before . . . at least not that I can tell, but it has changed me into something Mona says is a definite improvement. Mona, of course, is the key to the whole thing. Before I met Mona, my life was moving along and it had never occurred to me how much better it would be with someone like her in the center of it.

Maybe it's the same way with God. My life with Mona seems to be moving along just fine, but maybe it would be even better if God was in the center of it along with Mona.

That was, of course, almost word for word what Grandpa van Rijn told me months ago when I was having a hard time with Mona.

"Put her in the center of your life," he said.

Then, as an afterthought, he added, " . . . and you should do the same with God."

That final comment had been burning in my guts ever since.

Maybe it was time to have another chat.

"Let's walk over to the Met to see Grandpa," I said to Mona, "and then, if there's time, we can go to the MoMA and say "Hi" to Mom, too."

"Why not," she said. "It might be fun."

As we stood up to leave, my phone rang. It was Connie.

"Hey, Mikey," she said, "How're you doing with the face makeover?"

"What do you want, Connie," I said, as we stepped out onto Lexington.

"I thought you'd want to know they found gold in the tunnel up in Albany. It turned out there was 'buried gold' after all."

"No kidding," I said with my jaw dropping to the floor.

"Mona," I whispered to the side. "They found gold in Albany!"

"Professor Dick just phoned to bring me up to date," Connie continued. "They finished exhuming the little girl's remains this morning. When they uncovered her head, they found two gold chains with a small gold cross around her neck.

"He said it was ironic she was still in chains when she was buried, but, as he put it, 'The golden chains stood for freedom . . . as if Jesus had worn them on the cross so Goldie and everyone like her would never have to wear chains of iron again.'

"He also said he finds it ironic how the dead, like Goldie, are able to make history come alive for us today. He asked me to say 'Thanks' to you and Mona, and to everyone else who made the discovery possible.

"That's why I phoned," Connie said. "I thought you'd want to know."

"Thanks, Connie," I said. "I'll tell Mona. Bye."

When Mona prays she usually leaves me out of it. She just bows her head a little, closes her eyes for a moment and then she's done.

When I mentioned what Connie had said she stopped in the middle of the sidewalk, grabbed my hand, looked me in the eye and said, "Loving God, thank you for making everyone free. Show us how we can keep it that way. Amen."

Pedestrians were walking around us, staring as if they were driving past an accident on the expressway,

"Mona, couldn't that have waited until later?"

"No," she said, "it couldn't."

It was fifteen short blocks to the museum. The sun was shining and people were running around finishing off whatever errands they had put off for the weekend. As we walked along the Central Park side of Fifth Avenue, we could see trees that were already turning red or yellow in anticipation of the approaching autumn. There was a slight bite in the air; a welcome change from the stifling heat and high humidity that had suffocated the City earlier in the summer.

As we paused for the pedestrian light to change at 79th Street, a beat-up white Ford pulled to the curb and two men jumped out. The first one out was Doc but I couldn't quite place the other one. His face was strangely pale as if the skin hadn't seen the sun for a long time. It was, of course, Sam, freshly shaved and licensed to kill.

I figured it all out in the split second before Doc slammed into me like a special team's lineman smashing into a kick receiver who was too stupid to call for a fair catch. I went down like an express elevator, managing to roll sideways before my head slammed against the concrete,

Sam zeroed in on Mona and was already dragging her into the back seat of the car.

As I tried to block Doc from kicking me unconscious, I saw Mona spin around with her broken arm extended for maximum velocity. Her cast caught Sam flush on the side of his head. He staggered for a moment until Mona caught him full in the crotch with a kick strong enough to put a football through the goal posts at sixty yards. It would have taken a snow shovel to scrape him off the sidewalk when she was done

The pain in Mona's arm must have been terrific because, with her foot still in the air, she spun around and fell on the ground next to Sam, writhing in agony and screaming "Help! Help!" at the top of her lungs.

Some kid on a bike intentionally pedaled straight into Doc's leg and the two of them fell into a tangle of wheels, spokes, chains and handlebars. Sore as I was I managed to flop myself on top of Doc and, with the help of a few other pedestrians we managed to pin him to the ground.

Bombo, who was still sitting in the driver's seat, did what anyone in his situation would have done: He squealed off in a fog of burnt rubber. The two open doors slammed shut as he hit mach one and disappeared down Fifth Avenue heading south.

Over the years, we've all heard stories about New Yorkers ignoring cries of help from people being mugged or beaten just a few feet away. One reason for this might be apathy, some of it might be fear of "getting involved," and some of it might be the reasonable concern the attacker might pull out a knife or a gun and cause a world of hurt.

On this day, however, the pedestrians came through like champs. There must have been thirty or forty cell phones pulled out like six-guns at high noon. Some people were calling 911 and others were taking crime scene photos and videos to show to their families when they got home.

When New York's finest arrived three minutes later, they walked into a crowd of the finest New Yorkers I have ever seen in action.

Five of us received a free ride to the nearest Emergency Room to see who had been beat up the most

Unfortunately, Mona won the contest.

She had not only shattered her temporary cast, but X-rays showed she had dislodged her fracture and added a few more on top of it.

Sam took second place with a concussion and the possibility of permanent hearing loss in his right ear. Someone later told me he spent the next twenty-four hours curled up in a fetal position feeling as impotent as a steer.

I took third place with welts, bruises and a cut on my hand that took three stitches to sew up.

Doc and the bicyclist tied for fourth place with the sort of scratches and bruises normally associated with riders who dump their bikes during the *Tour de France.*

Actually, the biggest loser was the bicycle, which had been damaged so badly that an NYPD officer was compelled to put it out of its misery with a shot to the headlight.

Bombo was busted within the hour and all three men were issued stylish orange jumpsuits imprinted with personalized numbers on the front and the logo of the NYC Department of Corrections on the back.

Sarcastically speaking, it was the perfect end to a perfect week.

Chapter Twenty-Three

Groans & Sighs
Saturday Evening

After a few quick texts back and forth from the hospital, Robert and Chia took a cab across town to see how we were doing. What they found was that we were not doing very well at all.

"So," said Robert, "first you saved us from being kidnapped and now you've caught the kidnappers. Nice work."

"On the other hand," Chia chimed in, "it was Mike who got us into trouble in the first place, so it all sort of evens out."

I had never heard of a "hero-goat" before but I suppose there's a first time for everything.

Since Robert and Chia had the weekend free, they offered to help us back to our apartment and make sure we had something to eat for dinner.

Before receiving an honorable discharge from the hospital, however, there was one last thing I needed to do—I needed to put in a late afternoon call to "Sweet William."

"Where are you, Maurison?" he said when he picked up the phone and heard who was on the other end. "You blew it big time. Consider yourself unemployed."

"Wait," I said, "you'll never believe what happened to me this afternoon . . . ."

To his credit, he took the time to listen to my long, tragic tale.

When I finished he said, "Sure, and your dog ate your homework. Give me a break. That's the lamest excuse I've heard since Junior High School."

His tone changed when I told him I had the goods on Royal Throne.

"Oh," he said, sounding disappointed he wasn't going to be able to yell at me anymore. "Since you've got it, I'll have Junior stop by your place in an hour to pick it up. I already have your address. Thanks for finally getting around to doing your job. If it saves me big time I'll give you a bonus."

"That would be a bonus," I said lamely, probably because my painkillers were starting to kick in.

"By the way," I added, "when your father hinted at a way you could make a good living, was he showing you how to get a *head* in the world?"

William's response was two-fold: 1. There was silence, and 2. There was a click.

My painkillers were definitely starting to kick in.

Robert called a cab and I paid for it with an advance on my bonus.

We couldn't decide on what to have for dinner. Mona hurt so badly she felt like throwing up. My mouth was watering for something hot and spicy but my stomach felt as if it had been ruptured by the toe of Doc's boot.

Chia finally figured out what to have. She fixed warm tea and saltines for Mona and me while Robert scrambled up some eggs and cheese for the two of them.

Half-way through the scrambling the intercom buzzed. It was Junior from Sweet Spot. Mona buzzed him in and when he came to the door, I handed him the flash drive for "Your boss."

"He's not my boss," Junior said, "he's my father. Dad says running errands like this is the only reason I deserve to get an allowance. By the way, Mr. Maurison, and I don't mean to be rude, your face looks like my knee did after I fell off my motorcycle at the speedway last year. The knee still looks gross—would you like to see it?"

He started to pull up his pants leg but Robert stepped up and said, "It's okay, kid. We charge a fee for looking at knees like yours and, considering what your Dad gives you for an allowance, you probably couldn't afford it."

Junior got the hint, and after making sure the flash drive was safe in his pocket, he left.

"I'll make you a deal, Robert," I said after the door closed. "If you promise never to call me 'Knee-face,' I promise I'll never call you 'Bob.'"

"Sounds good to me, Spit," he said, using the nickname I'd been given as a kid.

Mona and I couldn't decide if we felt better sitting, lying down or standing up, so we kept popping up and down like Whack-A-Mole trying to find positions that were tolerable. Through it all Robert kept us entertained by telling us how the museum was going to welcome him back with a party on Monday.

"There's going to be a cake and a banner that says, 'One shoe off and one shoe on. Diddle-diddle dumpling, our friend Bob.'"

"You're kidding, right?" Mona asked.

"I can't be sure," Robert said, "but that's what the anonymous email threatened to do."

"Tell them what else it said," Chia prompted.

"At the end there was a PS: 'Sorry I didn't write sooner but I was tied up in Albany.'"

"I'm disappointed in them," I said." I would have thought the staff at the Museum of Modern Art would be more sophisticated than that."

"Well," Chia said, "to be fair, Adanya, the lady who usually guards your Mom in the Fifth Floor Gallery, sent Robert a text that said something like, 'Robert, you're so famous we're going to hang you on a wall by the front door and open it to the public as a special exhibit.'"

"I'd pay money to see that," Mona said.

"Me too," I said, "but since we have an annual museum pass we get in for free."

"Oh, good," Robert said. "That means you can come more than once."

"By the way," he added, "bring a hammer and nails and we can hang out together."

Chia quickly changed the subject.

"Mona," she asked, "have you heard from the library?"

"Yes," she nodded.

"They sent me a personalized, animated e-card. It showed a bunny standing inside a library putting her finger to her lips and whispering, 'Shhhh . . . Get Well' and then in a loud voice, shouting, "RIGHT NOW!' It was kinda cute in a nerdy, techie sort of way. I think it means they like me, otherwise the card might have had Darth Vader on it."

"That's the problem with being self-employed," I said. "I have to send myself a box of candy every time I get sick."

We were still too traumatized to say anything specific about what we had just gone through

267

together, but as friends whose friendship had deepened a notch or two over the past few days it was good to laugh about things that didn't matter

After we reassured Chia and Robert we were going to be okay, we said "Good-night" and "Thanks for the help."

We were beaten, bruised, sliced, diced, broken, battered and shattered.

Mona slouched on the sofa while I sat as rigid and straight as I could in a chair.

"What an interesting week," Mona said with her teeth gritted. "What do you think?"

"I found comparing various Emergency Room facilities and staff very interesting," I groaned. "How about you?"

"Personally, I found the contrasting police procedures and uniform styles particularly intriguing," she sighed.

"Next time," I said, "let's take another honeymoon instead."

"No thank you," Mona said with a slam dunk. "I'd rather spend the time watching network sit-coms on television. That way it wouldn't hurt when I laughed . . . ."

" . . . because," I finished the sentence for her, "there wouldn't be anything to laugh at."

"I love you, Mike," she said.

"I love you, too," I replied.

I was hurting so badly that, after I thought about it for a while, the suggestion of a full-cranial cast began to sound like a good idea . . . with or without the air holes.

After helping each other get ready for bed, Mona piled up extra pillows so she could prop herself and her arm as high as possible.

I found that lying on my side with my knees pulled up worked best. Unfortunately, my back was to Mona, so instead of a goodnight kiss we had to settle for one final groan and a sigh.

Chapter Twenty-Four

Sunday Morning Tune-Up
Sunday Morning

Mona slept better than I did. At least that's how it seemed when I woke up.

"Hi, hero," she said. "I've got breakfast ready for you, but you'll have to help me get dressed for church."

"Church?"

I said the word with an unintended grunt.

"You're going to church? You've got to be kidding. For the first time in your life, you have an airtight excuse to stay home and you're going anyway? That's borderline 'religious fanatic' territory. Next, you'll be moving into a cave in the Egyptian desert as a hermit . . . or hermitess . . . or hermitette . . . ."

271

"That's enough, Mike. Be careful what you say, because you're going to church, too, remember?"

She had me there, but it had been an infinite week ago since I promised I'd go to church with her this morning.

"Mona," I whined, "you can't hold me to something I said before . . . before everything happened. I can't go to church. I'm so sore I can't even get out of bed."

"You're going if I have to drag you out of bed with one arm," she said with more defiance in her voice than I wanted to hear.

"I'm a grown man and you're a grown woman," I said. "I don't tell you what to do and you don't tell me what to do. That's how good marriages survive. It's like a balancing act. We've got to do it as a team. There's no net and it's a long way down if we lose our balance."

"You're going to church if I have to drag you out of bed with one arm," she repeated.

I could feel myself starting to fall already.

Somehow, I managed to drag myself out of bed without Mona's help.

"What's for breakfast?" I asked. "And how did you fix it with one arm?"

"I put a bowl, a spoon and a box of "Toasty-Qs" on the table. You'll have to get the milk yourself."

I put a slice of bread in the toaster oven and traded the bowl, the spoon and the cereal for a paper plate and a butter knife.

"See," I said. "I did it all with one hand."

"I saw that," Mona said. "Nice work, but did you notice that sometimes you used your left hand and sometimes you used your right hand? You can't have it both ways. That's cheating."

"Mona," I said, "I would never cheat on you."

"You just did," she replied, "and that is why you're going to church, remember? . . . to get a final tune-up before Pastor Cheryl leaves for six months. Like you said, if you wait much longer your warranty is going to expire."

I ate the toast, got dressed, helped Mona put on her blouse and together we limped down the stairs and over to the bus stop on Fifth Avenue.

The ride to church took ten minutes and we were there fifteen minutes before the service started.

"I need to get a cup of coffee," I said.

"Then gulp it down," Mona said, "because you are not going to bring it into church . . . at least not if you want to sit with me."

I weighed the credit line of inhaling mouthfuls of scalding coffee against the debit line of second-degree blisters on my tongue and throat and decided to have a sip of water from the church drinking fountain instead.

For once, I was glad the church had been tastefully appointed with old-fashioned, solid wood, hard as nails pews. If the cushion on the seat had been any softer or thicker, I would have had to stand the entire hour to keep my back from going into spasms.

Mona was glad to have me next to her so she could rest her cast on my leg and take some of the weight off her sling and shoulder.

We stood for the hymns and I had to hold the hymnal and turn the pages for Mona. Even though she knew all of the hymns by heart, she seemed to feel that sharing the hymnal was somehow bringing us closer together. Unfortunately, I couldn't read the words because I was holding the hymnal too far away to see them.

"Why aren't you singing?" Mona asked.

"Because I love you," I answered, as my own shoulder began to ache from holding the hymnal at arm's length for so long.

"I love you, too," she said as she leaned her head against my shoulder.

As soon as my body felt the touch of Mona's cheek, the pain vanished. My shoulder suddenly felt so strong I could have lasted through another ten verses if there had been that many. As it turned out, four were just about all I could handle, and then, thankfully, we sang, "Amen."

Pastor Cheryl talked about God the Father and God the Son, Jesus, and how Christians believe they can't know the one without the other. She was finishing a sermon series on the Trinity and since I had missed the two about the Holy Spirit, I had a hard time figuring out what she was talking about.

Instead, my mind wandered back to the day Mona and I were married in the church chapel. I could see the chapel door off to the left and was half-tempted to sneak over and peek inside before the sermon was over. To do it I would have had to crawl over Mona to get out and with that in mind, I decided pews weren't such a good thing after all.

I leaned over to Mona and asked, "Where's the choir?"

She whispered back, "They've been off for the summer and will be back next Sunday. I know you'll want to come to hear them, right?"

Mona is very clever and finding ways to get me to stop talking during worship. With that question, she'd done it again.

Mona's normal routine after church is to head straight to the bus stop. This time, however, we stayed for the after-worship fellowship where they had coffee and cookies, along with carrot and celery sticks for those who were health freaks or had issues with gluten.

I was glad for the coffee. It wasn't as thick and black as the police variety but it could have been worse. In any case, it was free. Mona said at some churches it's called "Presbyterian Punch." I had absolutely no idea what she meant by it, but with enough sugar I suppose it could be turned into something that might taste a little like java-flavored Kool-Aid.

After Pastor Cheryl shook everyone's hand at the front door and said things like, "Thank you," and "Remember, next Sunday is my last one for a while," and "Tell Homer I missed him and hope he feels better soon," a hundred times in a row, she finally managed to break free and grab a cookie before they were all gone.

When the hosts began to clear away the goodies, we went down the hall to her office.

I knew the room well, having sat through three sessions of premarital counseling with Mona and Cheryl before we were married. It came as no surprise when the first thing the pastor asked us about was our wedding.

"Well?" she said, "How are things going? Did you survive the honeymoon with the sunburn and everything?"

Apparently, Mona hadn't had a chance to tell Cheryl how relieved we were when our two week fiasco in Europe was over so, instead, I simply said, "My sunburn didn't turn out to be as bad as I thought."

"Well," Cheryl said, "I know it was painful and you looked awful, but I've got to say you don't look any better this morning. Is this . . . I mean your face . . . is it a souvenir from last week?"

"I guess so," I said, realizing I had completely forgotten how disgusting I looked. "Mona has a souvenir of her own."

Mona lifted her arm up an inch or two and pointed at the cast.

"Just wait until you read about us again in this morning's paper," Mona said. "Our marriage has taken a real beating since we last talked, but it's all good. We're still in love and we haven't called it quits yet."

"So . . . ." Cheryl paused, " . . . why did you want to see me this morning? I only have a few minutes before I'm needed in a meeting."

"Go ahead, Mike. Tell her what you said."

"Oh, I just compared you to a car mechanic and said maybe we should have a post-marital tune-up before you leave town."

"Sort of a spiritual oil change, maybe?"

"Yeah, I guess. Maybe we're down a quart. It's been a rough week."

"Mike, when we talked about God before the wedding, you seemed uncomfortable and you let Mona do most of the talking. Did God show up at all this past week . . . I mean during any of the things you went through?"

There isn't a fortune teller in New York who could have nailed it any better than she did with that question. It occurred to me that if you take a car into the shop and you're not honest about what the problems and symptoms are, then it won't get fixed. With that thought in mind, I decided I might as well give an honest answer to the pastor's question.

"I can't tell for sure," I began, "but it seemed as if God was showing up everywhere, all the time. Maybe it was the stress or because I was so worried about Robert and Mona, but it seemed there was something or someone who gave me strength or encouragement when I needed it the most. Usually, Mona is the one who does this, but when she was kidnapped she wasn't there, so I guess I got it direct from the source or something like it."

"So . . . God seemed to be more real than before. Does that mean something to you?"

The questions were starting to hit too close to home so I hedged just a bit without abandoning the truth entirely.

"I guess it means that God won the debate. I guess it's . . . he's real to me, now, and even when I prayed I felt he was listening. It still doesn't make sense but that's how it happened."

Pastor Cheryl nodded, looked at her watch and found time to ask me one more question.

"In my sermon this morning I talked about how Jesus and God are a matched set; you can't know

278

God without knowing Jesus and you can't know Jesus without knowing God. Did that make any sense to you?"

"Not really," I said. "You asked if God showed up and I said, 'Yes,' but if you had asked if Jesus showed up last week I would have said, 'No.' I kept waiting for it but as far as I could tell it didn't happen.

"After surviving last week I think I'll concede the God part of it, but as for Jesus, except for being a good teacher who seemed to get things right most of the time, I'm not ready to say anything more one way or the other."

"At least not yet," Mona added.

"Mona?" Cheryl asked, leaving me as a *fait accompli* for a moment. "Is this a good thing for you? I mean for both of you?"

"Yes," she said. "God is real for both of us now and that's a good thing. A week ago, I might have thought Mike needed a complete transmission overhaul and I needed to have my brakes relined, but it seems like God used the past week to complete the necessary repairs in God's own way. I think we're good, thanks."

"Time is up," Cheryl said. "Would you like to have prayer before I go?"

Mona turned to me, letting me make the decision.

"No," I said. "Whatever you'd say, I think God knows it already."

When we got back to the apartment, I fixed tuna sandwiches for lunch. Mona said they were the best she ever had and both of us agreed that three hands are better than one.

I've said it a hundred times and I'll probably say it more than that in the years to come, but each day I love Mona more than I did the day before. How this is possible I have no idea, but none of it surprises me anymore. During the past week, for example, at least a dozen impossible things turned out to be possible after all.

As a result, I've adopted the motto, "You never know if something is impossible unless you try it."

I guess that's what Mona calls "walking by faith." If that what it is, then I guess that's what I'm starting to do.

There are, of course, plenty of mysteries still waiting to be solved. People who are looking for answers dump two or three of them in my lap every week. That's my job . . . looking for answers. After all, that's who I am: Mike Maurison—Private Eye.

Since July, however, I am also Mike Maurison— Married to Mona, That, more than anything else, makes me the luckiest guy in the world.

BOOKS IN THE MIKE MAURISON SERIES

Book 1
I Want My MoMA
A Year in the Life of Mike Maurison, Private Eye

Book 2
To Have and To Hold
A Month in the Life of Mike Maurison, Private Eye

Book 3
Treasure Hunt
A Week in the Life of Mike Maurison, Private Eye

Book 4
Smoke and Mirrors
A Day in the Life of Mike Maurison, Private Eye

OTHER BOOKS BY JAMES A. TWEEDIE

Long Beach Short Stories

The One Who Tells the Stories

All books are published by Dunecrest Press and are
available on Amazon.com as paperback or Kindle

Made in the
USA
Middletown, DE